Confederate Rose

by

Susan Macatee

Confederate Rose

COPYRIGHT © 2009 by Susan Macatee

Contact Information: info@thewildrosepress.com

Cover Art by *Nicola Martinez*
The Wild Rose Press
PO Box 708
Adams Basin, NY 14410-0708
Visit us at www.thewildrosepress.com

Publishing History
First American Edition, 2009
PRINT ISBN 1-60154-556-8

Published in the United States of America

"What? Are you telling me *you* were kissing *him*?"

His blood heated at the thought of her moving on to another man.

"I was tryin' to escape."

"By kissing him?"

"Aye." Anger flashed in her eyes. "And it was working until you came along and hit the poor lad."

He grasped her forearm and pulled her from the guardhouse. They couldn't stay here debating. "Come on, we've got to get out of camp. I fear I've compromised my cover."

"But what about Nate?" she protested. "You may have killed him."

Sighing, Alex knelt and felt for a pulse. The lad's breathing was regular, his pulse steady. "Reckon he'll be out for awhile, but aside from a nasty headache and some bruising, he should be all right." He rose and glanced into the guardhouse. "They'll reckon you clobbered him when he came for your dinner plate." He caught her worried gaze. "Now, let's skedaddle."

She nodded, but eyed him again. "Why are you dressed as a priest?"

"It's a disguise. I'm ministering to the Rebel soldiers." His eyes roved to the white vee of her bosom. "Button your shirt before we go. We don't want to attract any more attention."

Dedication

To my wonderful critique group: Jenn,
Marlene, Christine, Dee, Jeanmarie, Kristin-Marie,
Mary Ann, Nic, and Carolyn.

And to my editor, Allison Byers.

Thanks to all of you for loving my story.

Chapter One

Near Winchester, Virginia
March 2, 1863

Katie O'Reilly tensed as she stared at the swift-running stream. Trees cast long shadows across the rushing water, and the air held a biting chill. Her stomach emitted a growl, protesting not having had anything to eat since she'd departed earlier that morning. She yanked the empty canteen's cork to refill it before continuing the journey. As she neared the frigid water, her hands shook. Her mare, hitched to an oak tree, shook its mane and pawed the ground with the left hoof.

"I know, Morna." Katie glanced at the mare. "Allow me to complete me task, and we'll be on our way."

She bit her lip and turned back to the icy water. With heart pounding, she stretched the arm holding the canteen toward the white-foamed breakers.

"There's nothing to fear," she recited. Nevertheless, she planted her brogans securely on the bank.

A cracking sound, like a branch snapping, stilled the outstretched arm. "Morna?"

The mare whinnied. Katie whirled. A man stood beside the gray-white dappled horse. She reached for the butt of the sidearm tucked into her belt and pulled the brim of her felt hat down to conceal her face.

The man stood stock-still and didn't speak. Apparently, he'd hoped to make off with the pack or her horse.

He wore a greatcoat, so she couldn't tell if a uniform for either North or South lay beneath. Likely, he was a local civilian. A black wide-brimmed hat covered his head, under which thick chestnut-colored hair touched his collar. A full beard half-concealed his face.

Katie swallowed hard and tried to speak in her most commanding voice. "Are you lost, sir?" She gripped her pistol.

The man relaxed his stance. Perhaps he thought her too small to present a threat. He glanced from Katie to the mare, then downward to the mailbag she'd been carrying to camp.

Katie's hands clenched. While alone in the forest, she'd been careful to avoid enemy soldiers, thieves or worse, but this man had surprised her. *What was he doing here?* He looked again at the mailbag, then at her as if speculating on his chances of snatching it.

"Ye'll not be stealing me things!" She yanked at her belt, fingering the pistol.

The man didn't move.

A final tug freed the gun. Katie lost her balance on the ice-slicked edge of the bank and slid backward. She spun her arms and tried to stop the momentum but couldn't halt a fall into the swollen, rushing stream. Sharp needles of frigid water stabbed, sending a jolt through her body. Despite attempts to regain her footing on the rocky stream bed, she slid farther to where she couldn't reach the bottom.

Icy water closed over her head. Blindly, she lashed at the clear, cold breakers that tossed her from side to side. Forced up against a thick branch lodged between two rocks, she grasped it, trying to pull herself to safety, but her hands slipped.

God help, me! I'm going to die!

Strong arms clamped around her middle and pulled her backward against the current and out of the water. Limp like a rag doll, she allowed herself to be carried and deposited on the bank.

She curled into a ball, lungs heaving, and coughed up the water she'd swallowed. She lay shivering on the frozen ground and watched the man who'd rescued her shake water from his clothes and stamp his feet.

He glanced at their surroundings and swore.

Katie's heart pounded. *What possibly could this man want?* Whatever it was, she wasn't giving up anything without a fight. She reached out, grabbed his leg, and threw him off balance. He landed beside her with a thud.

"What do you mean to do?" she croaked.

The man gaped. "Son, I'm only trying to help—"

Self-protective instincts took over. She hauled back her fist and socked him in the jaw—her hand so numb, she didn't feel the blow.

"See here, boy!" The man tried to rise.

Katie slammed into him head first and sent both of them back into the stream.

"Are you some kinda lunatic?" he yelled. He grasped her waist and pulled her from the water, then straddled her while she gasped for air.

Cornflower blue eyes shaded by dark lashes regarded Katie warily. "Settle down. I don't intend to hurt you." His tone held an irritable edge.

Katie convulsed in a fit of coughing. "Let me up," she gasped.

"Only if you promise not to wallop me again." He rubbed his jaw. "For a scrawny fella, you pack quite a punch."

She stared up at the man. If he were a thief, why had he jumped into the stream to save her? He could've taken everything she had and allowed her to drown. She studied him. The man had a

3

handsome face, even though his hair was plastered to his head. Water dripped from his beard onto his shirt. He tried to look stern but failed. He spoke with a Southern drawl and seemed amused by the whole situation.

And he hadn't seen through her disguise.

"Sir," she said, "would you be so kind as to let me up now? I promise not to hit you again."

He rose with a grunt, then reached out a hand and pulled Katie to her feet.

"I've got a quilt in me pack. Me mare is just..." She looked around trying to catch a glimpse of Morna.

He inclined his head to the right. "Your pack's several yards that way. The current took us downstream. If I hadn'ta jumped right in after you, I would've lost you."

Katie eyed the stream and shuddered as she imagined being swept away.

"I'll get you back to your horse, then we can lead her up the trail to where my gelding is hitched. I've got two wool blankets in my pack, and my greatcoat is back on the bank where you fell in."

Katie nodded, still unsure of his intentions, but they were both soaked and shivering. They needed to get warm—and soon.

He led her back to the spot and bent down to retrieve his coat. The mare pranced and stamped when they approached.

Katie patted her mount, speaking softly to calm her. "There, Morna." She had been the foal of the original Morna, the first horse she'd owned and learned to ride on the O'Reilly farm. When the Yankees had taken her mare...She didn't want to think back to that horrible day.

She rifled through her pack, produced a patchwork quilt, and handed it to the stranger, but he shook his head.

"Wrap it around yourself. I'll use my blankets." He inclined his head toward the rise. "Just bring your horse and follow me."

Katie wrapped herself in the quilt, untied Morna, and followed the man's lead.

****

Alex Hart patted Rusty's flank, retrieved his blankets, and offered one to the boy.

The lad crinkled his delicate, freckle-spattered nose. "No, sir, I'm fine with me quilt," he said in a thick brogue.

"The hell you are," Alex scoffed. "Your teeth are chattering, and you're shaking. Take it."

The boy grasped his offering and used it to rub his flame-red, collar-length curls then draped the coarse, gray blanket over the quilt. Alex studied him. He was tall—coming to Alex's nose—and gangly, but he seemed a bit too pretty for a boy. The broad-brimmed hat he'd worn when Alex had first spotted him crouched by the water's edge had been taken downstream.

"What's your name?" Alex asked.

"Sean O'Reilly."

"I've been around enough military camps to reckon you're a soldier."

The lad blinked, hesitant. Clear, gray eyes seemed to assess Alex.

"I'm not a Yankee," Alex assured him.

"And you, sir..." The boy squinted. "Who might you be?"

He didn't see any harm in using his real name. "Alexander Hart, at your service."

"*Mister* Hart, is it? Yer not with the army, then?"

Alex sighed. When disguised as a civilian, he always had to be ready to answer this question, since most able-bodied men had enlisted in the army. "I'm a battlefield reporter for a Richmond newspaper, but I'm currently on leave."

"Richmond?" The boy's eyes narrowed. "Yer a long way from home, then."

Alex nodded. "My family has a farm near here."

The lad shivered, his brow furrowed.

Alex hoped the boy wouldn't read anything into his questions, except idle curiosity. But the lad's reticence about himself made Alex wonder about the pack. He didn't believe it contained only the lad's personal belongings. His guess that O'Reilly was a Confederate mail carrier could work to Alex's advantage. If he could gain the boy's confidence, he might be able to get that bag. His main problem would be hiding it until he could go through it for any useful information.

"I would suggest we both get out of these wet clothes before it gets dark."

"Yer not saying we should disrobe out here." The lad's eyes widened.

Alex glanced around. "There's no one here to see us but the horses."

****

Katie shivered. She couldn't undress in front of this man. He'd discover she was female. What was she to do?

"You must have some dry clothes in your pack."

"I need to be getting back," she protested.

"That can wait until you put on something dry. How far do you have to go?"

"From here, I'd be thinking about ten miles." She didn't want to give him any indication of her camp's location.

"The sun is setting. You'll never make it before nightfall."

She glanced at the reddening sky beyond the trees. Too late now to return to camp. She bit her lip, trying to decide what she should do. "Yer not suggesting we pitch camp right here?"

"It's as good a place as any. But sleeping out here in those wet clothes, you'll likely freeze to death."

Katie considered the situation. She could plead shyness. The cover of trees and her blankets would shield her, and he'd think nothing of her reservation to disrobe.

He rifled through his pack and extracted a dry, white cotton shirt and dark gray wool trousers. He dropped his blanket, pulled off his sack coat, and yanked down his braces. Her breath caught. He was going to undress right in front of her. Despite her strict, Roman Catholic upbringing, she couldn't tear her eyes away when he peeled off his shirt and undershirt. Gooseflesh rose on his muscular arms and chest. Coarse chestnut hair spread between taut, brown nipples and trailed down beneath the waist of his trousers. Katie bit her lip, heat rising to her cheeks.

"Aren't you going to change?" Hart spread his dry shirt over his chest.

"I...ah...yes, I'll get me clothes."

He sat and yanked off his boots and socks. When he stood and loosened his trousers, she averted her eyes. She busied herself in her pack, taking out a dry, muslin shirt, butternut britches, flannel underwear, and socks. She looked for a place where she could shield herself while she undressed. If she crept into the firs and draped a blanket and quilt across the branches, maybe while the man finished dressing, she could quickly change.

Katie spread the quilt and blanket across a pine bough as a barrier. After removing the sodden sack coat, she yanked off her brogans and socks, then slid down her trousers and underwear. She donned a spare pair of drawers, then pulled on the dry britches.

Her shirt and flannel undershirt were saturated,

too. After she removed them, she bent down to retrieve a dry shirt. A baritone voice, sounding much too close, called, "Get a move on, boy. It looks like a storm's coming in."

Hart peeked over the edge of the blanket. "What's the matter, son? You bashful?"

Katie gasped and clutched the shirt against her chest.

His eyes widened, then narrowed as he took in her form. "What the—?"

She didn't move as his gaze roamed over her body.

"You're no boy."

Chapter Two

Alex studied the young woman. Before she'd hastily covered herself, he'd glimpsed the small, white mounds of her breasts. Now he knew why she'd been so shy about disrobing.

His gaze fastened on her delicate features. Gray eyes fringed with reddish-gold lashes, a delicate nose, and rosebud lips complemented a rosy complexion spattered with light brown freckles. Now that he knew she wasn't a boy, he could appreciate the narrow waist and feminine features. She must have a reason for pretending to be male. Was she afraid of him, or did she hide her sex from the men in her camp?

She held the muslin shirt up as if it were a shield.

"Get dressed," he ordered. He turned away to give her privacy.

He wrung out his own wet clothing, then rolled it together, and shoved the soggy roll into his pack. The girl emerged from behind the blanket, wrapped in the quilt. She glanced at him, eyes wide.

"What's your name?" he asked.

She gulped, drawing his gaze to her slender, delicate throat. "I told you—"

"I mean, your *real* name."

She bit her lip. "Katie...Katie O'Reilly."

"Pleased to meet you, Miss O'Reilly."

"'Tis Mrs. O'Reilly."

"Pardon me." He studied her. She looked too young to be married. "Where's your husband, ma'am? In camp?"

"Aye...I've got to get back."

Now the disguise made sense. While serving as a lieutenant in Federal camp the first year of the war, Alex had encountered a woman who'd followed her husband into the military and pretended to be a man, sharing his tent. She wasn't discovered until ten months later when she delivered a baby girl.

He eyed the girl as she huddled and shivered in the blankets. Dry clothes would help, but they also needed a fire to ward off the cold. He didn't think building one here would be wise, though. They might alert a patrol. He didn't want to encounter soldiers of either army right now.

"On my way here, I noticed a cabin just up the road a spell. Didn't see anybody around. Reckon we could see if it's empty, or if someone's there, they might take us in for the night."

She frowned. "You can go if you want. I'll be just fine on me own right here."

"Reckon it'll get mighty cold tonight, ma'am."

"There's plenty of wood. I know how to build a fire."

"You're not afraid of alerting Yankee patrols?"

"I can take care of meself, Mr. Hart. I was doing it long before I signed on with the army."

"Your husband doesn't mind you being out here alone like this?"

She hesitated and gathered the quilt tighter. After lowering her gaze, she looked at him defiantly. "I do what I bloody well want. No man owns me."

Alex smiled. He'd seen women like her before. His own fiancée, a pampered Southern belle, had been willful and headstrong.

"Well, then..." He lifted his saddlebags onto his horse. "Reckon I'll be moving on."

"Are you going to the cabin then, Mr. Hart?"

"I'll see if I can spend the night there. Then first thing tomorrow, I'll head home."

"You never told me where your family lives, sir."

"Just south of Winchester, ma'am."

"You were on yer way home from Richmond, then?"

"Ah...no, I'm on my way south after a visit with my mother. She lives alone."

"You've no wife, then?"

"No, ma'am."

When she didn't say anything more, he turned to his gelding. After mounting, he turned back. "You're sure you won't come with me, ma'am?"

"No, Mr. Hart, you go on. I'll be fine here by meself."

He didn't like leaving her like this, especially now that he knew she was a woman. He'd been brought up to protect women. But he couldn't force her to go with him.

How could her husband allow her to travel alone with a war going on?

He tipped his hat in farewell, then turned his mount toward the road. He wanted to find shelter before it got dark. If that cabin he'd spied was deserted, it would be all the better for what he planned to do. Besides, he didn't like the look of the slate clouds dominating the sky.

****

Katie watched the man's horse canter down the wooded trail. Her mind flicked back to the sight of his naked chest, rippling with muscles. She bit her lip as sinful thoughts threatened to send her running after him.

She collected twigs to start a fire. Her fingers tingled when she recalled the feel of Rory's chest under her hands, while thoughts drifted to the last time they'd spent alone before the battle at Sharpsburg.

They'd been camped in Maryland in the woods outside the town with Federal troops close by. A battle seemed imminent. He'd come to the tent they shared, and they made love that night for the last time.

"Oh, Rory," Katie murmured. She placed twigs over the few logs she'd scrounged up. "I miss you so."

She dug in her haversack for a match and considered her predicament. The pile of wood seemed pitifully small, and the night would surely be long and cold. She'd have to pull out the axe and chop some more, but she was so tired.

Maybe she should have gone with Mr. Hart. He seemed harmless, and he *had* saved her from drowning. She shuddered when she recalled the feel of the water, like hundreds of icy fingers clawing, trying to pull her under.

After rummaging through the pack for the small axe, Katie removed it and searched for a sturdy branch she could chop up to get her through the night. With the sky so overcast, she could barely see a hand in front of her face. She had to get the lantern lit.

Patting Morna's flank, she squinted at the ground behind the mare. Something was missing.

"Where's me other pack? The mailbag!" She crawled on hands and knees around the tree where she'd left both packs.

"The bastard!" Could she still catch him? She'd have to find him before the overcast sky combined with the approaching nightfall made it too difficult to see. She gathered her things and saddled Morna. He wouldn't get away with this.

****

Alex picked his way down the trail. Dusk made it still possible to find his way, but he'd have to hurry. Guilt gnawed at him. Was it because she was a woman, or her youth and apparent vulnerability that gave him second thoughts about taking the pack? If she carried mail for the Rebels, he had an obligation to his government to obtain any information that would help the Union cause.

Plus, he'd asked her to come with him, and she'd refused. *Now, where is that damn cabin?* He'd seen the house clearly in daylight, set back a bit from the trail. He'd have to find it soon before impending nightfall made it impossible to find anything beyond the pines.

A cold gust of wind whipped around him, stinging his face, and intermittent drops of rain plopped on his coat. His luck could not have gotten any worse. Suddenly, the sky broke and sent rivers of icy rain down. His felt slouch hat and wool greatcoat gave only mild protection against the onslaught.

"Damnation! That cabin's got to be here somewhere."

Rusty turned his head and neighed in reply. No light shone through the surrounding wooded area. If the cabin were here, no one was home. Where had he seen it?

A clattering on the trail startled him. He turned Rusty around to face the sound. A rider on horseback approached rapidly. Alex grasped his revolver and tensed for whoever raced toward him.

When the stranger drew closer, Alex whipped the revolver out.

"You bloody thief!" the rider yelled in a high, strident voice. "Hand over me bag, you bastard!"

Alex kept the revolver before him but relaxed his grip. That crazed Irish Rebel had followed him.

She reined up abreast of him and didn't flinch at the sight of his drawn gun. Curls slicked against her head, and water dripped down her face.

She glowered at him, blowing out a puff of steam. Her breath came out in gasps, and the horse huffed.

"Hand over me bloody bag." She held out a

leather-gloved hand, oblivious of the revolver still pointed at her.

"What makes you think I have it?"

"Yer a thief and a liar. Give it here."

"You most likely left it back at the stream. Just didn't see it in the dark."

Her nostrils flared. "'Tis not *that* dark. You have it, and I want it now!"

Icy rain continued to pelt them. Alex bristled. She was keeping him from finding the cabin, where he could get dry and warm. As far as he knew, she didn't have a weapon. She'd lost her sidearm in the stream, and he hadn't seen a rifle among her belongings.

"Look, ma'am." He pointed the gun for emphasis. "I'm not going to sit here in this freezing rain and argue. When I find the cabin, you're welcome to come inside. I'll prove I don't have your bag. Fair enough?"

She bit her lip, apparently considering his offer. "If I don't agree, are you going to shoot me, then, Mr. Hart?"

He lowered the gun. "Of course not. I just wanted to convince you that we need to get out of this rain, before we both come down with pneumonia." He shook ice pellets from his hat and brushed his coat to emphasize his point. "We'll freeze out here."

She raised her hand. "Lead on, Mr. Hart. Is the cottage close by?"

"I believe it's just off this trail in a clearing beyond the wooded area. We can shelter the horses in a stable behind the cabin."

****

With no moon, Katie squinted to see through the dusky forest. Should she trust this man? He'd taken her mailbag and lied about it. Maybe no cabin existed. And he had a gun. Now was not a time to have lost her firearm. Too bad, for she was a good shot. Rory had seen to that. After they married and she moved to his farm in Virginia, he taught her to shoot and ride. Since losing him, she'd found the skills he taught vital to survival.

She followed Hart further into the forest and stared at the outline of his pack, wondering if the mailbag was in there. She couldn't imagine why he would take it. The bag contained nothing of value except to the Yankees.

Silence accompanied them as he led the way through the pines and dormant oaks. He stopped in a clearing, and Katie could make out the dark outline of a house.

"This is it." His voice barely audible. "The stable should be just to the right."

He dismounted and she followed. Their booted feet crunched ice into the frozen soil. Katie ran her hand along Morna's flank. She had to get her mare somewhere dry.

Hart handed over his mount's reins and stomped across the ice to the back of the cabin to investigate. Katie's pulse raced. The silence around them unnerved her. She half-expected a crazed man wielding a shotgun to burst from the dark house. Moments later, Hart appeared.

"Follow me," he commanded.

They led the horses to the darkened stable. He struck a match and swung his arm in a wide arc. Two empty stalls stood side by side, both filled with fresh hay.

"Let's get the horses out of the ice. I'll see to their needs after we get ourselves situated."

Katie bristled at being ordered about but could do nothing but agree. A solid roof overhead would feel wonderful. When not out on a mail run, she'd been accustomed to sleeping in a tent in the army camp. Morna nodded in apparent agreement as

Katie led her to the stall.

"This will do for tonight." He gestured to the corner of the stable. "The owners left a bucket of oats and some empty pails we can use for water. There should be a well around here."

Katie shook off her wet, wool clothing.

"Now, to see if the place is empty," Hart said. "You stay here, while I make sure no one's home."

"No," Katie protested, "I'm going with you." She was not about to let this man—whoever he was—boss her.

"I'm telling you to stay here," he ground out.

Since it was now too dark to clearly see his face, Katie could only tell from the tone of his voice he was angry. The only men she took orders from were the officers in the Confederate Army and President Jefferson Davis.

She pulled herself up to full height, which just reached his nose. "I assure you, Mr. Hart, I am perfectly capable of taking care of meself."

"You are, are you? Then just stay behind me and keep quiet. If there is anyone in there, I don't want to cause a confrontation."

The man was impossible. When Katie had joined the army with her husband, she'd been exposed to many hardships and threats from Yankee scum. After Rory's death, she'd continued to go into battle disguised as a man to avenge him and liberate the State of Virginia from Yankee tyranny. She refused to be bullied by this stranger. But if they could find shelter in the cabin, it would provide a chance to see if he had the mailbag among his things.

"I'll be quiet as a church mouse, Mr. Hart."

The sound of a holstered gun being pulled made Katie all too aware of her lack of a weapon. Hart moved slowly to minimize the crunch of his footsteps. She followed closely behind.

****

As much as he could in the darkness, Alex surveyed the small cabin ringed by bare oak trees.

The icy rain turned to fat, wet snowflakes. The woman drew up beside him, shivering. "Do you think anyone's in there?"

"We're gonna find out."

She hugged the wet, wool blanket she'd draped over herself. Her teeth chattered uncontrollably. "We could go inside and build a fire." She moved toward the door.

"Wait!" Alex pulled her back against his chest. He held his revolver in his other hand.

She turned and glanced up at him. "What are you afraid of? You think there are Yankees hiding in there?"

"Just be quiet!"

"I'll not be taking orders from the likes of you."

"In case you've forgotten, you promised to be quiet."

Her answer was an indignant huff.

The woman was impossible. She'd likely get them both killed. He had to lay down the law. "You'll do what I say."

She spat on the ground. "I don't know who yer thinking you are, but yer not me keeper, Mr. Hart."

Alex sighed. She was a hellbrand. A mere slip of a woman who swore, spat, dressed in britches, and didn't take orders. Just his luck to have come upon her by the stream. If it hadn't been for the mailbag, he'd have just continued on his way without her ever being aware of him.

He pushed her behind him.

"There's no call to shove me."

"If I could trust you to stay put and keep quiet, I could make sure it's safe to go inside." He lifted his revolver and gestured toward the cabin.

"Go right ahead, Mr. Hart, she said. "I'll stay right here. Without me sidearm, I won't be much help if there's a Yankee scout hiding in there."

He hoped she wouldn't be foolish enough to do anything to alert anyone who might be inside. "Can I trust you to keep quiet?"

"I'll not cause you any trouble. How would it benefit me? I'm cold and hungry. If that house is empty..." She stopped, apparently considering the possibilities.

The truth was, he didn't trust her for a minute, but they both needed to get warm and dry. Keeping his weapon raised, he crept forward, grasped the doorknob, and forced his way through the door. He tried to rely on his night vision, but the yawning blackness inside unnerved him. He pulled out another match and struck it against his boot.

The cabin consisted of two large rooms. Both appeared to be unoccupied. A large stone hearth sat to his left with a stack of cut wood beside it. A bed lay on one side of the fireplace, and a crude wooden table surrounded by four chairs stood in the center of the room. By the hearth sat a wooden rocking chair with the only other furnishings a couple of large wooden chests.

Alex crept to the open doorway that led into the second room. A gasp behind him made him tense. His heart raced, and he turned, revolver drawn, toward the sound.

Chapter Three

Katie gasped in appreciation at the sight of the cozy room, complete with stone hearth and cut wood piled as if awaiting their arrival. "Now isn't this just perfect."

Hart advanced and raised a warning finger to his lips. "I told you to stay put," he whispered hoarsely.

"'Tis cold and wet outside." She spread her arms and added, "Seeing as no one's here..."

"I haven't checked in there yet." He pointed toward the doorway of a second room.

"Go right ahead, Mr. Hart. I'll be staying right here."

"That's what you told me the last time," he growled. "I almost shot you."

Katie frowned. Whatever was wrong with the man? Did he really expect her to stand out in the cold, icy rain, when they had this wonderful cottage all to themselves? Come morning, she'd just take her bag and be on her way, as far away from him as possible.

She motioned for him to proceed. With a final glare in her direction, he struck another match and disappeared into the other room.

While he was occupied, she shook out the blanket she'd draped over herself and rubbed her wet hair. She had a bundle of candles in the pack. Even if they didn't find any lanterns, they'd have plenty of light. Once they got a fire started, it would be quite comfortable. Much better than spending the night by the stream.

Hart emerged from the second room with a lit oil lantern. "Reckon we've got the place to ourselves, unless the owners show up tonight." He set it on the table. "There's another lamp in the kitchen, and I've found a bottle of lamp oil. I'll go back to see what else I can find."

"We should start a fire." Katie gestured toward the hearth. "We need to dry off and get warm. It'll give us more light, and we can dry out our wet things." She met his gaze over the lantern. "I've got some food in me pack. And the owners may have left something behind that I can cook."

"You cook, do you?"

"Aye, of course I can cook. Are you daft?"

"I don't know. You dress, spit, and swear like a man. How does your husband feel about that, Mrs. O'Reilly?"

Katie dropped her gaze as the hollow pain of loss swept over her. Bloody hell! Why did the man have to bring back memories of Rory? The six months he'd been gone seemed like just a few weeks. The pain was still raw.

She glanced up at Hart, who watched her, his head tilted in speculation. Well, she'd not give him any information to indicate her widow status.

"Me husband doesn't own me."

"So you've told me, ma'am."

"Do I offend you, then, Mr. Hart? I'm not a genteel Southern belle like yer used to."

He frowned. He'd told her he wasn't married, but that didn't mean there wasn't a woman somewhere waiting for him.

He turned away and approached the hearth. He glanced back over his shoulder. "I'll start a fire. You take that lantern into the kitchen. Light the lamp on the table out there, and see what kind of supplies you can find."

Katie bit back a retort. *Did the man think her a*

dolt? And did he never stop giving orders? But, instead, she nodded and grasped the lantern's handle. Once they had some light, she could look for the bag. She'd not be leaving here without it, nor shirk her duty by allowing the mail to fall into the hands of this thief.

She set the lantern on a large, rectangular table, flanked by six chairs. Had this family lost everything like the O'Reilly's had when the accursed Yankees had invaded their farm? She sighed at the memory. She had to forget the past and focus on her task.

She found the oil flask on the table beside the other lamp, and a large box of matches. She lit the wick, producing a glow that enabled her to inspect the entire room. A sturdy oak cabinet contained earthenware bowls, plates, cups, and saucers. A stone hearth, identical to the one in the other room, held a cast iron rod. Two large, lidded pots hung from it, and two tin buckets stood on each side. She'd have to locate the well, so the horses could be watered.

A pantry revealed the owners had left a few supplies. Canisters holding flour, sugar, what looked to be baking powder, cornmeal, and a few coffee beans lined the nearly barren shelves. She opened and shook each of the canisters to be sure there were no weevils. With the lack of abundant supplies, it appeared they had a chance to grab what they could whether they voluntarily left or were forced to leave.

Katie stepped into the other room. A fire crackled in the hearth. Bright yellow-white flames licked at the cut wood. The inviting scent of wood smoke drew her forward.

Hart glanced over his shoulder. "Reckon this will help." His gaze drifted over her from head to toe. She must look a fright. But so did he.

He looked at one of the wooden trunks against the wall. "Maybe we could find something in there to wear until our clothes dry out."

Katie turned toward the massive oak chest. "'Tis as good a place to look as any." She retrieved the lantern from the table and approached the wood box.

Hart moved to her side, then lifted the lid while she held the lantern above. She eyed the contents as he rummaged through them. He pulled out a few dresses of muslin and cotton, aprons, and linens. When he got to the women's cotton underthings, he blushed. Katie felt her face flush in embarrassment as well.

"Maybe the men's things are in the other chest," he reasoned.

A quick check of the contents produced only a few tattered quilts and blankets. No other clothing.

"Reckon I'll have to make do with what I'm wearing and the wet bundle in my pack," he said.

"It would seem they've taken everything that could be of use to them," Katie said. "The women's clothing is all summer weight. There are no flannels at all."

"Which means, they likely won't be coming back anytime soon. Seems we have the place at our disposal."

Katie nodded and wondered if that bode them well or ill.

"I'll fetch those buckets and see to the horses," he said. "While I'm gone, you can change and start hanging our wet things by the fire."

He went out through the kitchen entrance, clanging the empty buckets against the door.

After he'd gone, Katie sat on the floor for a few minutes and fingered one of the cotton dresses. The simple one-piece wrapper with a starched white collar and row of pearl buttons down the front could double as a work dress. A paisley design of white over burgundy patterned the material. She absently brushed her hand over it, as she recalled the last time she'd worn such a dress.

She and Rory had been living in Virginia on the farm his family owned. She'd first met him in New York, where she and her family—newly arrived from Ireland—lived in a shanty town. He'd regaled her with stories of his family farm. Horses, open space, fresh air...it had sounded like heaven.

After a brief courtship, he'd asked her to marry him. She'd readily agreed and moved with him to Virginia.

After the war started and the Yankees had come, taking so much from them, Rory and his brother enlisted in the Confederate Army. Katie, refusing to stay alone on the farm, discarded her female attire to enlist as a man.

She hadn't worn a dress since.

The chance to stay with Rory had been worth it. She only wished he could have seen her garbed as a woman one more time before he'd died.

She wiped a tear from her cheek, rose, and held up the dress. Aside from being a wee bit short, it looked to be a good fit. She searched through the chest and pulled out a white cotton chemise, a pair of drawers, and a petticoat. She could sleep in the chemise and wrap herself in one of the quilts for warmth.

She hurriedly stripped off her wool sack coat and remaining clothing, rubbed her damp skin dry with one of the blankets, then slid the cedar-scented undergarment over her head.

Padding barefoot to the fire, she shook out her wet things. She spotted the two chairs by the small table and pulled one toward the fireplace, then arranged her clothing over it, so it could dry quicker. She slid the other chair forward.

She rifled through her pack and pulled out the spare set of clothes she'd rolled into a wet bundle. She draped them over the second chair, then did the same with his, noting the bag of mail was nowhere in sight. Hart had to have it hidden somewhere. Knowing this may be her only chance to go through his things, she knelt before the crackling fire and searched the contents of his pack.

****

After Alex fed and watered the horses, he rubbed them with a gunny sack he'd found in a nearby corner. Before heading back to the cottage, he checked on the mailbag he'd carefully concealed in a pile of hay. Come morning, he wasn't sure how he'd sneak it by the Irish hellbrand. He was convinced she wouldn't hesitate to clunk him on the head or even steal his revolver to get her bag back. He'd have to be careful.

Entering through the darkened kitchen, he placed the empty pails by the hearth. He approached the doorway leading into the second room and the sight that greeted him stopped him cold.

Katie O'Reilly, dressed in nothing but a loose, white cotton chemise, knelt by the fire going through his pack. She turned toward him, eyes widening. The glow accented her curves through the light material. He clenched his teeth and willed his body not to respond.

He stepped into the room. "Just what the hell do you think you're doing?"

With one arm covering her chest, she lunged for the quilt on the floor. She wrapped herself in it before she rose to face him.

"Well, speak up. What are you doing going through my things?"

Her pale cheeks turned a becoming shade of pink. She lifted one white, bare arm from the quilt to gesture at the clothing drying by the fire. "Now didn't you tell me to hang yer things out to dry?"

Alex grimaced. He *had* told her to do that. But he hadn't expected her to go through his pack. "So I did," he admitted.

She slipped her arm back into the quilt and lifted her chin. "'Tis an apology I should be expecting, Mr. Hart."

"Apology? *You* were going through *my* things."

"Because you ordered me to see to yer wet clothes."

Alex didn't think he'd win this argument. "Very well, ma'am. I apologize if I've offended your fine sensibilities in any way."

She straightened and hugged the quilt, eyeing him regally. "I accept yer apology, Mr. Hart."

"Well then." He hesitated and dropped his gaze. Her wide eyes drove his thoughts to ideas best left alone. That and the knowledge of what little she wore under the quilt. He cleared his throat. "I suggest we bed down for the night."

"Not until you get yerself out of those wet clothes."

His brows shot up. "I beg your pardon?"

"Ye'll surely not be sleeping in those wet things. 'Tis by the fire ye'll be needing to hang them."

His gaze settled on the clothes draped over the two chairs. Steam rose from them. "But those clothes aren't dry yet."

"Ye'll not be needing clothes to sleep." She grinned mischievously. "We've plenty of blankets."

He hesitated. Stripping off his wet clothes *would* feel good.

But he couldn't in front of a lady, even if she *were* married.

She blushed as if reading his thoughts. "I promise I won't peek."

His skin flushed at the thought of those eyes watching him, but not entirely out of embarrassment. He curbed his overactive imagination and wondered what Mr. O'Reilly would do if he caught them together. "Let's get some sleep then," he finally said.

They retreated to opposite sides of the hearth. She settled onto the bed and wrapped herself in additional blankets. After turning away from him toward the outside wall, she pulled the quilt over her head.

Alex glanced at the fire and decided to throw a few more logs on before he retired. Satisfied the fire burned steadily, he rolled out a pallet by the hearth. He quickly stripped down to his drawers. They were slightly damp, but he wasn't about to sleep naked with a woman in the room. After he draped his clothes over the rocking chair, he wrapped his length in the blankets piled on the rug by the fire, then settled into a fitful sleep.

****

Katie opened her eyes, startled until she remembered where she was. Glancing about, she noted red embers still glowed in the hearth and illuminated the long shape of a shrouded body. He didn't stir except for the barely perceptible rise and fall of blankets around him as he breathed. At least the man didn't snore.

She gathered her quilt, rose, and padded toward the curtained window. The cold floor against the soles of her feet sent shivers down her spine. A grayish light filtered through the cotton panels. She parted them. The sight forced a gasp from her parched throat.

Chapter Four

Nothing but white greeted Katie. About two feet of snow blanketed the ground around the cottage, and a slew of large, fat flakes descended from the sky. She felt like the house was the only thing in existence inside a giant white ball. She couldn't even distinguish the stable from the rest of the countryside.

She glanced toward Hart who still slept soundly. Should she wake him? It would be best to let the man sleep. They couldn't leave until the snow stopped. She'd get the fire going, dress, and see what she could find to cook.

A short time later, Katie pushed the saucepan of water into the fireplace to heat. She glanced over at Hart still completely wrapped in the blankets she'd piled onto the floor last night. Only his thick, chestnut hair and the top half of his face escaped the coverings. His eyes twitched beneath his lids as if he dreamed. Long dark-brown lashes nearly skimmed his chiseled cheeks. He showed no other sign of movement.

Her gaze drifted over his long, lean body beneath the blanket then to the rocking chair, where he'd draped his clothing. She bit her lip as she speculated about what, if anything, he wore. One bare foot slid from the edge of the covers.

Katie turned back to the fire, stabbing at the logs with the cast iron poker. The only naked man she'd ever seen had been her husband.

She lifted the pan from the hearth. Mr. Hart moaned. She set the pan on the stone floor and studied him.

He jerked awake suddenly, reaching for his revolver. His eyes widened, apparently at finding himself on the floor, before he settled back onto the blankets. His gaze drifted over Katie's form, lingering a bit too long on her exposed ankles.

She brushed a hand over the blue-checked muslin apron that protected the burgundy dress she'd found in the chest. Although the skirt was short, it fit everywhere else and would do until her clothes dried.

"Yer finally awake, I see." She gestured at the fireplace. "There's not a kettle to be found in the place. In me cornboiler, 'tis tea I'm brewing. Thought to fry up a hoecake fer breakfast."

Hart rose to his elbow. The coarse, gray blanket slipped downward, exposing his broad, muscular chest, sprinkled with fine chestnut colored hair.

He eyed her. "You look different."

Katie's face flushed. "'Tis the dress from the chest."

He rose from the pallet wrapping the blanket around him. She caught a flash of his white drawers. He carefully placed his revolver on the pine table between them.

"Yer clothes must be dry by now." She waved toward the rocking chair.

He nodded. "You kept the fire going."

His drawl sent a pleasant tingle down her spine. Although she'd lived in the South for five years and now lived in a camp full of Confederate soldiers, the timbre of this man's voice captivated her. She longed to hear him speak again, but he seemed reticent.

"Stoked it this morning, I did," she explained. "Thought to use it to cook breakfast and added a few logs to the hot embers, since the hearth in the kitchen is damp and cold. I've tea brewing now if ye'd care fer some."

"You're very resourceful." He lifted his wool trousers from the chair. "Reckon I should make myself decent first."

Katie's cheeks flamed. "I'll be turning me back, if you want to dress."

"Thank you, ma'am.

She kept busy at the fire, contemplating the sight of Mr. Hart's lightly tanned skin, and the taut muscles she'd glimpsed when the blanket had slipped from his shoulders.

Sucking on her lower lip, she lifted the lidded cornboiler from the fire and set it at the base of the stone hearth to keep warm. Then she poured the batter for the hoecakes into the greased frying pan.

She flipped the cake. Satisfied it was fully cooked, she deposited it on the plate she'd set on the floor. Using the knife from the haversack, she cut the large cake into two.

"I'm decent," Hart murmured.

She turned from the fire to face him.

He smoothed the collar and cuffs of his shirt, then adjusted his braces over his shoulders.

Dropping her gaze, Katie placed the plate on the pine table and dug into the canvas pack for spare utensils. After arranging the cups she'd found, she poured tea from the cornboiler she'd left steeping by the fire.

He sat at the table and grinned. "Sure smells good. You did all this while I was asleep?"

"Aye." She shrugged. "Thought you'd be hungry when you woke."

He flashed a lopsided, boyish grin.

Her pulse quickened. He was handsome and a charmer, but who was he really? Although he spoke with a Southern drawl, it didn't mean he wasn't affiliated with the enemy. She sucked on her lower lip as she poured the tea.

"I've got some sugar in me haversack, I do, but

I'm afraid we'll have to do without cream."

He flashed the grin again. "Ma'am, you sure know how to take care of a man."

****

Alex watched Mrs. O'Reilly's retreating back. She disappeared into the kitchen to look for a bottle of syrup. The dress enhanced her already pleasing appearance, although he preferred his women a bit rounder in the hips and bosom. His thoughts drifted to Annabelle. Hair the color of wheat, blue-green eyes, full bosom and hips accented by a tiny waist, Annabelle was the epitome of genteel womanhood in the South.

Growing up together, they became engaged before he'd gone north to further his education. But when he'd returned, rumors of war had started circulating. She'd called off their engagement when he'd refused to enlist in the Confederate Army. Called him an abolitionist and worse.

Although Annabelle had been adamant he fight for 'the Cause', would she have fought beside the men as Mrs. O'Reilly did? He couldn't imagine it. Annabelle's idea of patriotic duty was attending military balls and soirées, or teas with the ladies where they discussed what hardships their men endured or bemoaned the lack of male companionship. He couldn't imagine her setting her dainty feet in an army camp.

Mrs. O'Reilly swept back into the room, interrupting his thoughts. She set a small glass bottle on the table. "'Tis all I can find."

Alex eyed the clear bottle half-filled with amber-colored syrup.

When he didn't move, she said, "Eat. Ye'll be needing yer strength."

"Pardon me?" He reached for the bottle.

"Ye've not looked outside, I take it."

"Outside?" He glanced at the gauze-covered

window.

The sky appeared dark. After glancing at her, he rose to investigate. When he pulled back the curtain, the sight before him sent his stomach plummeting. Snow covered everything as far as he could see and continued to fall from the lead-colored sky with furious resolve. "This can't be. I have to get out of here today."

He thought of the dispatch in his pack. He had to get to the Federal camp five miles east of here. How could he do that now? Then there was the matter of Mrs. O'Reilly's mailbag, still hidden in the stall with the horses.

He turned from the window.

She seemed to read the look on his face. "Ye'll not be leaving here today."

He pushed a hand through his hair. What was he to do now? He was trapped in this cabin in the middle of nowhere with a lovely Irish Rebel. Meanwhile, he had a Federal dispatch in his pack he'd be unable to deliver but would certainly incriminate him if it fell into Rebel hands.

The woman picked up her knife and fork but continued to look at him. She pointed to his plate. "You should eat. Ye'll feel better."

"I don't think so." He took the seat across from her. He stared at his meal, unable to summon back his appetite.

"Starving yerself won't make it go away," she said between bites.

"You're right." He picked up the utensils she'd set for him. "It does smell mighty good."

"Go ahead," she urged. "Fill yer stomach."

When she smiled at him, all thoughts of the blizzard outside were forgotten. He lifted his fork and shoved a hunk of syrup-coated hoecake into his mouth. Chewing slowly, he savored the sweet, hot morsel and quickly shoved in another mouthful. He murmured in satisfaction. If nothing else, the woman could cook.

"When yer finished," she said, "I'll be cleaning up here, and you can be seeing to the horses."

He nodded. Good, he didn't want her near there. If she found the mailbag...They finished their meal in silence, then he trudged through the knee-deep snow to the stable.

****

Later, with nothing to do but while away the hours, Katie produced a deck of cards from her pack.

"I assume you play poker, Mr. Hart."

He raised his brows. "Why, yes, I've been known to play more than a few hands."

She smiled and set the deck on the table.

"Would you care to deal?"

He pulled out the chair opposite her and lifted the deck, expertly shuffling as his gaze drifted over her.

She flushed and concentrated on his hands as he finished and dealt the cards.

"I'm guessing you learned this game in camp." His gaze caught hers.

She nodded, then lifted the cards, trying to suppress a grimace at the horrible hand she'd been dealt.

"You of course know, poker is a betting game." He glanced at his cards, then back to her. "What are we wagering?"

She shrugged. "I'm low on funds. Me pay should be waiting when I get back to camp, but until then..."

"We don't have to make a monetary wager." He studied his cards.

Katie bristled. *Just what would be the meaning of that?* An idea occurred.

"The loser has to cook dinner tonight." She eyed him, holding back a grin.

32

"Is that so?" He smiled. "What makes you think I can cook?"

"What makes you think you'll lose?"

"All right." He leaned back in his chair. "We'll go for three out of five. Whoever loses, cooks dinner tonight."

"Agreed." She didn't know how good a card player he was, but since she'd planned to prepare the meal tonight anyway, what did she have to lose? Unless he turned out to be a horrible cook.

As the afternoon wore on, Katie managed to win the first two games. He won the next. Her throat grew dry and painful as her voice turned raspy. She drew the shawl tightly as the room took on a chill.

"I'm thinking we should build up the fire." She glanced at the hearth. "And a cup of tea would be nice, right now."

"You're cold?" His brows drew together in a frown as he glanced at the fire. "It feels a bit warm in here to me."

Katie tried to respond but was shaken by a fit of coughing. Her throat burned and a twinge of pain pinched the bridge of her nose.

"I'll throw another log on, then boil water for tea." He rose from the table. "But you only won two games. I'm holding you to three wins."

Katie smiled. Once he left the room, she pressed her palm to her forehead. She wasn't feeling well at all. Hopefully, a hot cup of tea would ease the pain. Dry, wracking coughs shook her body, increasing her distress.

Once Hart had stoked the fire and she held a cup of tea, she sipped gratefully, enjoying the warmth and soothing liquid sliding down her parched throat.

Hart took the seat across from her again, and they resumed the game.

****

Alex watched Mrs. O'Reilly as they played another hand. Although she tried to put on a front that all was well, he noted her skin had turned paler than usual, and even though she drank hot tea and the fire burned steadily, she still clutched the shawl around her as though she were freezing.

He wiped his brow, tempted to remove his coat. A few times she convulsed into a fit of coughing, but insisted she was all right.

He won the next game, but she beat him in the third with a full house. He rose resignedly from the table.

"Reckon I'll see what I can find in the kitchen to cook."

She laughed, but it sounded raspy. "I've already searched the kitchen, but they must have a root cellar beneath the house. We'll see what we can find."

He grabbed a lantern, and she followed him to inspect the cellar. Turnips, cabbages, carrots, potatoes, squash and onions—enough for what little time they would have to spend here—filled the small space.

"You could make soup," Katie said.

"Soup? With nothing but vegetables?" He wrinkled his nose.

Katie laughed. "I've got a bit of salted beef in me pack we could add."

"That sounds better," he relented.

Although he was to be the cook, Katie assisted him with preparations, then settled down to rest while he tended the pot simmering in the hearth.

****

After the meal, Katie's throat felt a bit better, although her headache continued to grow. She decided she'd wash the dishes, while he tended to the horses, then she'd retire for the night. She set a pot of water on the hearth to heat, then gathered the used dishes into a pile on the table.

Mr. Hart had seemed very upset when he'd first seen the snow. Although she'd expected it—after all, she was upset by it, too—she had to wonder just what he'd been thinking. If he were a war correspondent, surely with the snow, there'd be nothing going on for him to report anyway.

She tapped her fingers on the table. While she waited for the water to heat, maybe she could try looking through his pack again. He'd caught her the last time. She couldn't afford to have that happen again, but she needed to know more about him. Eyeing his leather pack lying beside the rocking chair, she bit her lip. Should she dare? She'd find herself in a great deal of trouble if he came back just as she was going through the pack again. She glanced toward the kitchen and made her decision. She'd face the doorway and listen for the sound of the back door. As soon as she heard him open it, she'd quickly put everything back the way it was, and he'd be none the wiser.

She took a deep breath and rose from the table. Her head throbbed dully and sweat broke out on her brow at the small effort. Sidling over to the bed with one eye on the open doorway, she sat and opened the pack. She found a few handkerchiefs, a comb, pencil and journal, and a sealed letter. She pulled the paper out, eyes on the door, then glanced down. The envelope was blank. She ran a thumb across the seal.

The sudden sound of a door unlatching startled her. She shoved the letter into the pocket of her apron and quickly closed and pushed the pack into place beside the bed.

She rose and approached the hearth, checking on the dish water. When Hart entered the room, she was bent over the wash pan testing the temperature. Another spurt of coughing wracked her body, forcing her to sit. Nausea rose up, but she took a few deep breaths, forcing it down.

"The horses are fine," he said, "but the snow is about two feet deep and still coming down hard. It looks like we'll be stuck here for awhile."

Katie nodded. She glanced about for towels to lift the pan from the fire.

"I'll do that, ma'am." He reached for the towels. "Where do you want it?"

"The table will be fine." She indicated the spot where she'd laid out a dry towel.

He carried the hot wash pan to the table and set it down. When she placed the dishes into the water, she noted his glance toward his pack. Seeming satisfied, he proceeded to remove his wet hat and coat.

Katie raised her eyes heavenward. Thank goodness she'd heard him before he caught her again. She could never have explained her way out of it this time. After patting the letter tucked inside the apron pocket, she turned away so he wouldn't see her blush of shame. She hoped he didn't go through his pack looking for it.

She wondered who the letter was for. With no name on the envelope, she could only assume he was to hand deliver it to someone. He'd said he wasn't married. Could it be to a lover? But surely he wouldn't hand deliver a letter to someone he knew. Curiosity ate at her.

Katie watched him from the corner of an eye as she scrubbed the dishes. He leaned toward the hearth warming his hands. They were large, with long, tapered fingers but looked like they'd seen their share of hard work. She scoured the cast iron frying pan she'd cooked the hoecakes in and fantasized about those hands holding her, roaming over her body.

She bit her lip and scrubbed harder as shameful

thoughts filled her mind. She had to stop this. She didn't know this man. They were trapped here alone until the snow ended. And Rory—God rest his soul—had been dead six months now.

She had to stop thinking about Mr. Hart. She treaded down a dangerous path. Taking a deep breath, she watched his back. He turned from the fire, his gaze locked on hers, and she momentarily found herself lost in his blue eyes. She'd been without the loving comfort of a husband for so long. And although she lived in camp surrounded by men, she had to pretend to be one of them. Only her brother-in-law, Patrick, and a few others knew she was a woman.

Mr. Hart wasn't like most of the men she came into contact with every day. He seemed more refined. Like the officers.

Was it that quality that made her insides quiver?

Although she'd loved Rory, she'd never felt that way with him. He'd been an escape. A way out of the slums of New York City. As an immigrant who had never ventured beyond the city, Virginia had sounded like a strange, exotic place. More like Ireland. Anything was better than slaving for twelve hours a day at the yarn factory, while living in a cramped tenement shared with her parents and two brothers.

Living on a farm in Virginia had seemed like a dream come true. All she had to do was marry Rory.

She looked up to find Hart watching her as she finished with the pans.

"Is there something I can do fer you, Mr. Hart?"

He smiled, and her breath caught. Did he know what that smile did to women? Especially lonely ones?

She gulped and tried to force words past dry lips. "I should be seeing to me mare."

"She's fine. And, believe me, you don't want to go outside right now."

She nodded, but her heart raced furiously, and her face heated. She had to get out of this room. Escape, even into a snowstorm was her only hope. But would even that stop such sinful thoughts?

He placed both hands flat on the table.

She stared at them and swallowed. All rational thought fled as her head pounded and a sudden wave of dizziness caused her to sway.

"Easy now." Hart rushed to Katie's side, easing her into one of the chairs. "Are you ill?"

She lifted a hand to her forehead. "The room is spinning." She glanced toward the ceiling and couldn't seem to focus her eyes. A wave of nausea gripped her. "The wash pan!"

Hart shoved the pan, still filled with dishwater, in front of her. She heaved the contents of her dinner into it.

She couldn't be getting sick—not now. She lifted her hands to clammy cheeks. "I think I'll be needing to lie down."

Hart helped Katie to her feet. "Let's get you to the bed."

They worked toward it, but the distance seemed to lengthen. Katie feared she'd never reach it. Her legs felt like noodles, unable to support her weight. She collapsed into his arms. He lifted and carried her to the bed.

"I'm so sorry," she said.

"Sorry for what?" His eyes held concern.

"Fer getting sick."

"That's not your fault, ma'am. Just rest and allow me to take care of you."

He drew the quilt over her, and she drifted off to blessed oblivion.

Chapter Five

As Mrs. O'Reilly slept, Alex occupied himself with a game of solitaire while keeping watch over her. After awhile, a plaintive voice broke the silence.

"Oh, Rory," she murmured. "I'm not feeling so good."

"Ma'am?" Alex focused on her pale face.

"I don't want to die. Not like this."

He leaned closer, grasping her small hand.

"I love you, Rory, but I'm not ready."

"Mrs. O'Reilly?"

She responded with another moan. Could Rory be her husband? Either dreaming or delirium caused her to call another's name. He reached over and brushed wet hair from her forehead. He should have noticed earlier she was sick. Perhaps the illness had been brought on by her fall into the stream.

How much more bad luck could accompany him on this assignment? He was already late for his rendezvous at the Union camp. Now, he was snowbound with this Rebel Irishwoman.

He ran a hand through his hair. What was he to do? One thing was for certain, he couldn't leave her here like this, Rebel or no. He'd have to stay and see her through this illness. Otherwise, she'd likely die. He refused to have that on his conscience.

Hopefully, once she got back on her feet, the weather would permit them to ride away from here and go their separate ways. All he could do for now was care for the horses and her and hope the available food held out.

When he released her hand, it fell by her side.

Moisture had popped out on her forehead, and Katie's wrapper appeared damp. A lump formed in his throat. He had only one option. He'd have to remove her clothes to help cool her. His fingers fumbled on the buttons of the wrapper. Once undone, he worked her arms out of the sleeves, rolled her onto her side, and pulled off the garment.

He eased the brogans from her, exposing stocking clad feet, narrow with high, delicate arches. Reaching beneath the legs of her drawers, he loosened her garters and rolled the stockings down over the curves of her slim calves and ankles. Willing his body not to respond, he continued to remind himself she was married. He would remain a gentleman.

After drawing cool water from the well, he used a towel to sponge Katie's face, but heat continued to radiate from her body. Her chemise was plastered against her skin. Although he hated to completely undress her, it was the only way to cool her down.

Reaching under her chemise to her waist, he loosened the drawers and pulled them off. Hoping he'd never have the opportunity to meet her husband, Alex worked the undergarment over her torso to her armpits. Positioning her arms over her head, he peeled the garment off her, leaving her naked.

Her white breasts—the mounds adorned with strawberry nipples he'd only glimpsed at the stream—drew his gaze. Feeling aroused at the sight, he diverted his attention by jumping up to look for more towels. He soaked them in the bucket and draped her body from head to toe.

Although he could no longer see her body, the vision of her breasts and narrow waist, as well as the slight curve of her hips and triangle of red curls between her slim thighs stayed with him.

He glanced at her face. The wet towels seemed

to have calmed her, but her skin still felt hot. Would she survive? If he got sick, too, they'd both be doomed.

****

Katie hauled two more buckets of water into the medical tent. Doc Newberry and his assistants worked on a young soldier stretched across the table, preparing him for surgery. Blasts from cannon fire reverberated through the woods surrounding the camp, and the pungent scent of gunpowder tinged the air.

She watched in horrid fascination as the men cut away what was left of the poor man's bloodied trousers. The coppery scent of blood and the knowledge of what they were about to do caused beads of sweat to break out on her brow. They drew markings of where they had to cut to amputate the leg, and she swallowed hard. The man screamed for them to stop, and a chorus of moans echoed around her.

She felt an insistent tug on her trousers that wrenched her gaze away from the horrid scene. "Boy, may I please have some water?"

"Aye, sir."

The gaunt man's brown eyes looked huge and sunken against his pallid skin. She searched for a ladle, then scooped water for the thirsty soldier.

After drinking his fill, his gaze lifted toward the tent opening. Another blast shook the ground. "It's hell out there in the field, son."

"Aye, that it is." Katie smiled, trying to give the man some comfort. "Is our side winning?" She feared hearing the answer.

The man shook his head. "I can't say for sure, son. I'm jest glad to be out of there."

Katie nodded. Rory was out there. And his brother, Patrick.

She gulped, desperately needing air. Even the

41

acrid odor of gunpowder would be better than the stench of blood and death. She left the tent, swallowing, trying to fight the panic of having her husband engaged in the fierce battle. What would she do if he didn't come back?

She gazed toward the clouds of thick smoke rising above the battlefield. Stretcher bearers approached carrying a man between them on the litter. Katie moved aside to permit them entrance to the medical tent.

"It's too late for this one," Jacob said. He was a sixteen-year-old drummer boy, a tall, strapping lad who'd been assigned to help bring in the wounded. He gazed at her with large hazel eyes. "He done expired before we could get him here."

"Are you sure?" Katie asked. "Maybe one of the doctors should be having a look."

The other man, a dark-haired, stocky private named Nate, who'd been assigned as a hospital steward and nurse—as was she—shook his head. "Too late, Sean, reckon we should just put him over yonder under the apple tree."

Katie stared at the man on the litter, and her heart lurched. A hard lump rose in her throat making it difficult to swallow. "Please," she said, "put him down here." She indicated a spot a few feet from where they stood.

After glancing at each other, the young men nodded and gently laid the litter down, then stood back and eyed her nervously.

Her knees gave way. She sank beside the body. "You knew who this was."

They removed their caps. Nate said, "Yes, Sean. We know he's your brother. We just couldn't think of a way to tell you."

Nodding mutely, she turned her attention to Rory. Running her hand along the stubble on his cheek, she allowed her tears to fall freely.

****

"Rory, what am I to do?" she called aloud.

A strong hand rested on her shoulder. "Mrs. O'Reilly?"

Her eyes popped open. Hart gazed down at her. Where was she? Realization hit her. She took in the walls of the cottage—the bed she lay on. The fire crackling in the hearth. She'd been back in Sharpsburg—the day she'd lost her husband.

"You called out for someone named Rory," Hart explained.

"Aye. Me husband."

He nodded. "You were restless just before."

"A dream." She glanced around. "I feel a bit woozy. How long?"

"Since we've been here?" he asked. "Five days."

"Five days?" She couldn't believe it. "Have I been delirious the whole time?"

"Mostly, you slept. You've had a high fever. I wasn't certain you'd live through it."

Katie tried to rise onto her elbow but fell back, exhausted.

"You're not strong enough to get up. Whatever you need, I'll get it for you."

This stranger had been caring for her the entire time. After glancing beneath the quilt to discover she was completely naked, Katie glanced up at him accusingly. "What have you done with me clothes?"

He frowned. "Your clothes were soaked with sweat. I had to undress you."

"And you were unable to find another undergarment?"

"It was easier this way. You had no sense about you, ma'am."

"Easier fer what?" she ground out.

"To care for you."

She pulled the quilt up to her chin. "I'm not insensible now. I'll be needing something to wear."

"Yes, ma'am." He rifled through the chest, producing another white, cotton chemise. He held it up for her inspection. "This is all I can find."

"It will do." She snatched the garment.

"I did what I had to do, Mrs. O'Reilly." His face colored. "On my honor, I did nothing improper. You would've died without my care, ma'am."

Katie considered his words. The thought of those large, strong hands touching her intimately, sent shivers over her bare flesh.

"I'd assist you, but I reckon you'd prefer I left."

She swallowed. "I think that would be best, Mr. Hart."

"I'll tend to the horses while you make yourself presentable—but don't try to stand yet. I'll help you when I come back."

She inclined her head in agreement, grateful for his offer of making himself scarce while she dressed. But did she have the strength to place her feet on the floor? After he left, she slowly pushed herself to a sitting position. Her head felt as if it would float away. She lifted the cedar-scented chemise and slid it over her head and arms, breaking into a sweat at the small effort.

Lying flat on her back, she pulled the garment down her torso, arranged the chemise, and waited for the dizziness to pass. She stared at the oak ceiling beams and realized if it hadn't been for Hart, she'd have died. On the other hand, she wouldn't have fallen into the stream, caught a chill, and gotten sick in the first place. She'd be back to camp by now. The whole misadventure was his fault.

She glanced toward the window. The sky was a clear, pale blue. Bright sunshine sent beams through the window glass, warming the cottage. How long had it been since the storm had ended? He said she'd been ill for five days. She tried to envision Hart caring for her all that time, tending to her every intimate need. Her cheeks grew hot even as she felt the urge to use the chamber pot. He'd told her to stay in bed, but the thought of his assisting her was too embarrassing. If she could manage to stand beside the bed, she could take care of her needs before he returned.

Gingerly pushing herself to a seated position, she waited until the room stilled. She took a deep breath, easing her legs over the side of the bed. She allowed them to dangle before shoving further with her hands and bottom and sliding her toes to the wood floor. The chill against her bare feet sent a jolt through her system. Her weakened limbs trembled, and nausea rose in the pit of her stomach.

She transferred her weight to her legs, tightening her fingers on the bedpost for support. She straightened to a standing position, but the room lurched around her. Her legs could not support her. She collapsed to the floor in a heap.

****

Alex strode back up the path he'd shoveled three days before. The horses seemed to have weathered the sudden storm well. He'd been exercising them daily since the snow had ended.

How long would it be before Mrs. O'Reilly could ride? Though she was a Rebel and he could very well jeopardize his mission by staying, he couldn't bring himself to leave her alone. She wouldn't survive without someone to care for her until she fully recovered. While tending to her, he'd forgotten she was the enemy. But now that she was well, he had to leave. He couldn't delay his assignment any longer.

Entering through the kitchen, he first dislodged the snow from his brogans, then sat the bucket of fresh water he'd drawn from the well by the kitchen hearth. Once he saw to Mrs. O'Reilly's needs, he'd start a fire to heat the broth left from the stew they'd eaten earlier.

A glance at the empty bed drew his gaze to the floor where Mrs. O'Reilly lay in a heap of cotton, bare white flesh, and the quilt she'd dragged with her. He rushed to her side where she lay moaning.

Kneeling, he tilted her face toward him. "I thought I told you not to get up until I came back."

"I needed to use the chamber pot," she explained.

Relieved she didn't seem hurt, he replied, "You're not strong enough yet. When you need something, you call me, and I'll take care of it."

"Aye. All right."

She still wasn't herself, the independent courier he'd found by the stream. She'd given in too easily. Good, it would make his job of getting her well simpler. He helped her take care of her needs, then settled her back onto the bed.

"Now you stay put, while I get a cooking fire going in the kitchen. It's time you got something in your stomach to help get your strength back."

After tucking the quilt around her, his gaze fastened on her smile. Her eyes seemed huge against her pallid face. Food and rest would bring the roses back into those cheeks. He contemplated how he would bring the feisty, spirited red-head back to health. He strode to the hearth to start the fire.

****

Katie settled back, listening to the comforting sound of Mr. Hart busying himself in the kitchen. It reminded her of when she was a wee lass back in Ireland and her mother cared for her when she succumbed to the occasional childhood illness.

She hadn't seen her parents or brothers since marrying Rory and coming to Virginia. Now, his parents were dead—his father killed by Yankees when he'd tried to keep them from plundering his farm. Rory's mother had later died of a broken heart. Rory's brother, Patrick, served in the 2nd Virginia regiment with her. She'd never met Rory's two sisters, who'd married and now lived out west.

With her own family still in New York City and her regiment camped miles away, she was completely on her own. If not for Hart, she would surely have died.

Why *had* he stayed with her? Perhaps guilt for causing her illness in the first place was the reason.

Whatever kept him with her, she couldn't help but be grateful. Hopefully, once she fully recovered, they could travel together to locate her regiment. Her mind drifted to the whereabouts of the mailbag. Maybe he hadn't taken it, after all. But what else could have happened to it?

Hart interrupted her thoughts when he entered the room carrying a steaming bowl.

Katie inhaled the aroma. Beef broth. Her stomach growled in anticipation.

He set the bowl on the table. "I reheated the broth, but fear we're stuck with the vegetables left in the root cellar, unless you've got more dried beef strips in that pack of yours. There's not a chicken to be had in this place."

"Is that so?" The vision of his butchering a chicken brought a smile to her face.

"I found some preserved jars of fruit in the pantry. If you can keep this down—" He indicated the broth. "—I'll spoon some out for you, along with a cup of tea."

"That would be lovely, Mr. Hart." She rose to a seated position.

He raised a warning hand. "No getting up. I'll bring the broth to you."

Katie watched, amused, as he carried a small side table and set it by her bed. He pulled a chair beside it, then brought the bowl, spoon, and two towels and set them on the table.

After pulling his chair up close to the bed, he

laid a towel against her neck, cradled the bowl inside his other hand, and lifted it close to her face. He took the spoon in the other.

She reached for the utensil, but he shook his head. "No, ma'am, you just sit and relax."

Settling back against the pillow, she watched his hand as he spooned the broth from the bowl, then lifted it to her lips. She accepted his offering, savoring the warm liquid that slid down her parched throat. The whole time he served her, she found herself transfixed by his vivid blue eyes.

After several spoonfuls, she giggled. "I've never been fed before by anyone but me mother."

"This is a pleasure, Mrs. O'Reilly. After all, I feel somewhat responsible..."

"For me being ill?" she finished.

"If I hadn't startled you by the stream..."

"You blame yerself fer me falling in?"

He nodded.

"But you saved me life. If you hadn't jumped in, I would've drowned."

"I would never have allowed that to happen."

"I'm terrified of water." She shivered at the thought. "Ever since I was a lass."

Hart studied her. "What happened to make you afraid?"

"I was at the river's edge with me brothers. Two British soldiers appeared and frightened me, so I fell in. I was only seven and had never learned to swim. I nearly drowned. Me brother pulled me out."

"What did the soldiers do?"

Katie shrugged. "They just stood there and laughed at us."

His face clouded. "And you never learned to swim later?"

"I couldn't." She dropped her gaze, unable to explain her terror.

"But when you came to this country..."

"Aye." She nodded. "We came over when I was fifteen. I was ill the entire voyage and never so glad to see dry land again."

"I'm certain the trip was difficult for you."

"'Tis fortunate for me you're such a strong swimmer, Mr. Hart."

"Call me Alex."

"I'm not thinking we should be all that familiar."

He grinned. "I'm spoon-feeding you. Like it or not, we've become intimately familiar."

Gooseflesh rose on Katie's bare arms. She wanted very much to be familiar with this man. Sinful thoughts of what she'd like to do with him entered her mind, and she couldn't help but smile.

"Alex is a very fine name. You can call me Katie."

Chapter Six

March 15, 1863

Days later while sharing a companionable breakfast of oatmeal, Katie made a mistake. As she regained her strength, she'd started pulling her own weight, but Alex's gentle care during the time she'd been deathly ill had caused her to lower her guard.

"How is it a young lady like yourself ended up in the Confederate ranks?" Hart lifted his tea cup, awaiting her answer.

"I went along with me husband and brother-in-law."

He took a sip of his tea. "I have a hard time believing your husband would allow that."

"He tried to talk me out of it," Katie said, remembering, "but there was nothing left fer me. When I lost..." She halted. She couldn't bear to voice the words.

Hart frowned. "What is it?"

She shook her head. "'Tis nothing." In truth, she couldn't bear to reveal any more of what the Yankees had done that day. "After burying his mother," she went on, "Rory and his brother, Patrick, decided to join the rebellion. Me family lives in New York City. I refused to go back there."

"So, you joined up, too."

"Aye." She nodded.

"But why disguise yourself as a man? Women serve as laundresses and nurses."

"I wanted to fight." She quickly looked away and started to gather the used plates.

"You fought in battles?"

Did she detect admiration in his eyes?

"Aye. Rory taught me to shoot on the farm. I fought by his side in many skirmishes."

"Any major battles?"

"We were at Sharpsburg, but I'd been assigned to hospital duty. Rory and Patrick were in the ranks." The hurt flashed back making it difficult to speak. "That's when I lost him."

Hart's gaze narrowed. "Lost who, ma'am?"

"Me husband," she whispered. The memories of that day still felt raw. Holy Mother of God, she hadn't meant to say that. She bit her lip in frustration.

"But you told me your husband was waiting for you in camp."

"Aye," she admitted, "I didn't want you to know I was a widow."

He nodded. "You were afraid of me. Afraid I'd take advantage of you."

"You are a stranger, after all. How was I to know you'd be so honorable?"

His complexion reddened, and he ducked his head. "I quite understand, ma'am." He rose and helped her stack the remaining plates and cups. "I'll get some fresh water to heat for dish washing." Moving to the door, he scooped up the empty bucket by the hearth and disappeared outside.

****

That afternoon, Alex brought the bucket to the well and drew fresh water. Although several days of sunshine had accomplished a fair amount of melting, the snow surrounding the cabin was still deep. The food supply ran low, as well as feed for the horses.

He returned to the cabin and hung the filled bucket in the hearth. He turned to Katie. "It's too late to leave today, but I'm going to see if the road is passable so we can possibly leave early tomorrow."

51

Her eyes widened. "But 'tis so cold." She tightened the wool shawl she wore around her shoulders.

"We have to get out of here as soon as we can. I'll just hike out to the road."

She nodded slowly but obviously didn't like his idea. "Please, be careful." She reached for his hand.

Her touch set his heart racing. He decided a hike out in the cold would do him a world of good. He shrugged into his greatcoat trying to get the image of her rosebud lips and short red curls out of his mind.

Since learning she was a widow instead of the married woman he thought her to be, he'd had a hard time keeping his thoughts away from how he'd like to thoroughly kiss those lips.

"Take care, Alex," she said as he opened the door.

Glancing back, he nodded, then turned quickly away.

The snow was not only deep but had a thick crust, making each step a great effort. The farther he moved away from the warmth of the cabin, the harder it became not to turn around and head back to the warmth. To her.

Concentrate. One step after another. He had to make it to the road, if they were to survive. A biting wind hit him full in the face, stinging any exposed skin. Cold penetrated his wool gloves and numbed the tips of his fingers.

He plodded on. His feet and legs grew more deadened by the minute. No longer able to feel his fingertips or nose, he finally reached the road on a ridge overlooking the cabin.

His pounding heart sank. No way could their horses get through this. They had to pray for a warm up to melt a lot more of the snow before attempting it.

Dejected, he started back toward the cabin.

****

Katie's stomach fluttered as she watched Alex's form grow smaller. No longer able to see him, she moved away from the window. She'd clean up the dishes to take her mind off him.

Although she occupied herself scrubbing and drying the plates, cups and cutlery, her thoughts strayed to Alex—his compassionate eyes, those chiseled cheeks framed by his fine chestnut beard, and large, work-roughened hands that captivated her. Her cheeks warmed, and butterflies flitted about in her stomach as she recalled the image of his broad, naked chest. *What would it feel like to rub my hands over his hard muscles?*

Holy Mother of God! She made the sign of the cross over herself. She had to stop these sinful thoughts. Rory had only been gone six months. She cannot allow this man to affect her so.

She dried her hands on her apron and paced the length of the kitchen. If the road were still impassable, they may be trapped for who knew how much longer.

She moved to the window and scanned the horizon. Nothing. Maybe he'd found a way out, and she wouldn't have to worry. Back in camp, she was surrounded by men every day.

Glancing out the window again, she could make out something moving closer. His gray coat and black hat contrasted against the bank of snow. When he neared the door, she opened it. His weight pushed into her, and she struggled to keep them both upright. Shivers wracked his body.

"Mother of God, yer frozen!" she gasped. Pushing all her strength against him, she guided him into the room by the fire.

She helped him out of his hat, gloves and coat, wrapping blankets around him.

"It's impossible." He rubbed his hands together and leaned toward the hearth.

"What?" Katie tensed, fearing his report.

"We can't get out yet. The horses wouldn't make it."

"Bloody hell!"

His body shook, and his teeth chattered uncontrollably.

"We have to get these wet clothes off you." Katie settled him in the rocking chair and helped him remove his wet brogans and socks. Snow crusted on his wool trousers.

"Loosen yer braces," she ordered.

He flashed an indignant look but complied.

"Stand up, so we can get these off."

"You're going to watch me undress?" he asked, eyes wide.

"'Tis better than having you catch pneumonia."

He sighed, stood, and loosened his trousers.

She peeled them over his drawers. Ordering him to sit again, she pulled them off.

"The drawers, too."

"For God's sake, woman!"

"They're wet. I won't have you gettin' sick. We've plenty of blankets you can cover yerself in." She turned her head to allow him privacy. When she turned back, he'd wrapped the blanket around his waist.

"Shirt, too," Katie said.

Shooting an exasperated glare at the ceiling, he pulled off his shirt and undershirt, leaving his chest bare.

Katie bit her lip. She itched to run her hands over the chestnut hairs covering sculpted muscle. "Wrap yerself up, and lie here by the fire."

She helped him enshroud himself in the blankets and lie on the pallet on the floor. His skin was so cold. Even with the heat of the fire, he didn't stop shaking.

"Come here." She stretched beside him and gathered him into her arms. "I'll help you get warm."

She snuggled against him, draping the blankets over them both. His shivering subsided. Comforted by the warmth of the fire and the feel of his hard body, she drifted off to sleep.

****

Alex awoke with a start. Where was he?

His arms were wrapped around a body. A soft, warm body. He opened an eye. Katie lay pressed against him, sleeping. Her lips were parted, and her breath lightly fanned his face.

The last thing he remembered was her trying to warm him. Although she was fully clothed, he found himself completely naked under the blanket.

He needed to slip from her embrace and get into his spare set of clothes before she awoke. He tried to untangle himself from her arms, but she snuggled closer.

He was already aroused, and her movements made things worse. Her rosebud lips parted enticingly close to his mouth.

"Good Lord." He groaned. Heat rose in his body, and he brushed his lips over hers, warm and smooth as silk. Sweet as maple syrup.

She opened to him, kissing him back. Her hand rubbed his bare back, and she pushed herself closer.

Her eyes opened, widening, but she didn't stop. She writhed against his arousal. Wanting to get rid of the layers of clothing separating them, he tugged at the buttons of her wrapper, loosening it to her waist. Only her chemise lay between him and her warm, inviting skin.

He cupped one of her breasts through the fabric. He kneaded the soft mound through the material, and her nipple grew hard. Pulling the neckline of the garment lower, he feasted on the white flesh.

His breath hitched, and he hardened. He took her lips again, then nibbled his way to her silky throat, earning delightful gasps from her. He reveled in her softness and feminine scent.

"Oh," she murmured. "Oh, Rory."

Alex froze.

****

As soon as the words escaped her lips, Katie realized what she'd done.

Alex stiffened in her arms. He pulled away, using the blanket to cover his nakedness and stood.

"I'm sorry, Alex." She sat up and closed the wrapper over her chest. "Rory was the only man I've ever been with."

He turned away, the blanket firmly wrapped around him. He gathered his clothing. "Reckon I'll be getting dressed, ma'am, if you don't mind."

She rose from the floor. "Of course, I've things I can be doing in the kitchen."

Once she was out of his sight, she buttoned her wrapper. Tracing her tongue along her swollen lips, she could still feel his kiss. After Rory, no other man had touched her. Most of the soldiers in camp thought she was male. Only Patrick and a few others knew her identity. Pretending to be a man for so long, she'd forgotten the joy and desire of being a woman. Or maybe she wanted to forget, since she'd lost Rory.

She brushed her hand over her womb and felt empty. She should have had Rory's babe to raise. If not for the Yankees...But Rory and the wee babe were dead and buried. She now only lived to kill Yankees.

Attracted to Alex as she was, she had to be careful. She'd been devastated when she'd lost her babe, and even more so when Rory had died at Sharpsburg. Although lonely, she had to guard her heart. She couldn't bear to have it shattered again.

Chapter Seven

Confederate Camp near Berryville, Virginia
Same Day

Captain Maurice Bernard sat on his bunk, a pipe spewing aromatic cherry-scented tobacco between his teeth. His aide ushered Sergeant O'Reilly inside for a requested interview. O'Reilly saluted. Maurice indicated for him to sit on a chair across from him.

"I'm still waiting for my coffee," Maurice snapped, turning his attention to the aide.

"Yes, sir. Right away." The aide scurried off.

Maurice removed his pipe, his attention back on the sergeant. "What may I do for you, Sergeant?"

"Sir." O'Reilly twisted his cap in his hands. "Request permission to look for me brother."

Maurice stroked his handlebar mustache. "Your brother?"

The sergeant squarely met his gaze, and Maurice could read the anger in the man's eyes. He settled back recalling the punishments he'd meted out to the Irishman when his temper had gotten out of line. No doubt, the sergeant thought Maurice to be an unfair taskmaster, but if it took a whip to bring his men under his control, so be it.

"Is your brother a civilian?" Maurice asked.

"No, sir. He's an enlisted man in this company. Private Sean O'Reilly."

"Then where is he that you have to search for him?" Maurice's blood heated. Why *did* this man have to drag him into his family's affairs?

"Sir, he's been sent on a mail run to Richmond and is long overdue. I fear something's happened to the lad."

Bernard leaned forward, resting his hands on his knees. "Permission denied, Sergeant."

"But, sir..." The color rose in O'Reilly's cheeks.

"I can't have my men traipsing all over the place searching for lost relatives." Maurice raised a hand. "Your duty lies here."

"But, sir, he's me baby brother. I promised me ma on her deathbed that I'd look after him."

Maurice shook his head. "Absolutely not."

O'Reilly balled his fists in his lap.

Maurice hoped the man wasn't foolish enough to desert his post. "If I find you've left this camp without permission, I'll hunt you down myself and have you shot as a deserter. Is that understood, Sergeant?"

"Aye. I'm sure you would, that," he murmured.

"What was that, Sergeant?"

Maurice stared the Irishman down.

"'Tis nothing, sir. I'll be returning to me duty."

With his hands still fisted, O'Reilly rose stiffly and exited the tent.

Maurice stroked his mustache again. That boy was nothing but trouble—had been since the day he arrived in his brigade. He would definitely need to be watched.

Maurice leaned back savoring the pipe's aroma.

Where is that damn aide with my coffee?

The aide appeared as if on cue at the tent entrance, a cup of steaming liquid in his hand. "Sir?"

Maurice scowled. "Why does it take you so long to do anything, you worthless twit?"

"I'm sorry, sir." The aide rushed forward, hefting the cup. In his haste he spilled some of the liquid on Maurice's table, just missing a stack of official reports.

"You idiot!" Maurice spat.

"I'm sorry, sir. I'll clean it up." The young man's face turned beet red. He shuffled papers trying to spare them as he brushed the liquid away.

"Just get out!"

"Yes, sir." The aide scurried off.

Maurice took a deep breath. "Why must I be surrounded by imbeciles and incompetents?" He took a sip of his chicory brew to ward off the chill morning air and calm his nerves. His gaze slid to the letter on the edge of the table. Fortunately, it had escaped the spill. He lifted the scented parchment and read it again.

March 10, 1863
My Dearest Maurice,
I will accompany Daddy on a business trip to Winchester in two weeks. While there, I plan to visit you in camp. I long to see you again. I recall how handsome and dashing you looked in your uniform before you left for the war.
Expect me soon.
Your Loving Fiancée,
Annabelle

Maurice crumpled the letter, tossing it to the ground at his feet. What the devil was his future father-in-law thinking? Annabelle's place was at home, awaiting his return, not traipsing after her father during wartime to visit an army camp.

Unfortunately, he couldn't do a thing about his strong-willed fiancée, at least not until after they'd wed.

After that day, everything would change. His last wife, Muriel, had been a sweet little thing when he'd courted her, but once they'd married, she'd turned into a harlot. At the time, he'd been young and blinded by a pretty face. She'd had no inheritance as Annabelle had, but foolishly he'd thought he was in love. Muriel seemed to cater to his every whim, only drawing his wrath and punishments on rare occasions. But behind his back, she'd been a different woman. The day he'd caught her in the arms of a traveling salesmen, he'd taken justice into his own hands. After venting his rage, he'd buried Muriel and her lover in unmarked graves and left the house, never to return.

He'd lost everything he'd worked so hard for, because of that foolish bitch. Annabelle was his chance to start over. He was fortunate her former fiancé, the son of a plantation owner, had shirked his duty, and she'd given him the mitten. Maurice was in the right place at the right time to comfort her. She was headstrong, but he had experience with his father's slaves. He wouldn't make the mistake he had with Muriel. He'd grind Annabelle into submission.

His father had gambled his plantation away, leaving the family penniless. Maurice would never forgive him. If he ever had the opportunity to kill the bastard who'd spawned him, he surely would. His mother had died three years ago, the rest of his family had scattered.

Yes, Annabelle was his ticket out of his penniless state. Once he'd married her and had hold of her inheritance, he'd keep her under his iron hold.

****

"Sir." The aide poked his head into the tent. "The company is assembled and awaiting inspection?"

"Yes, I'll be right along." Maurice grinned. He always enjoyed inspecting the company.

After shrugging into full uniform, he strolled before the group of men. He felt such a sense of power commanding a company of one-hundred men.

They stood at attention, awaiting his approval.

He surveyed the group. *Who will I wreak my wrath on today?*

His gaze rested on Sergeant O'Reilly. The man actually squirmed but kept his gaze straight ahead.

"Call roll, Lieutenant," he ordered.

The officer strode down the line, calling names and getting responses.

"Ben Harrison," the lieutenant called. This was met by silence.

Maurice scowled. "Where is Private Ben Harrison?"

"Didn't see him this mornin', Captain," a private volunteered.

Maurice seethed. "What's your name, Private?"

"Carl Wilson, sir."

"Private Wilson, I want you to find Private Harrison and bring him here."

"Yes, sir." The soldier scurried away.

Maurice paced, planning what punishment he'd mete out to Ben Harrison, once the man was found.

****

Later in the day, Private Harrison was ushered to Maurice's tent. He was partially dressed, no vest or coat, the whites of his eyes streaked with red. His hair was disheveled and his skin pale.

"Private Harrison. Why weren't you at roll call this morning?" Maurice demanded.

The private's eyes darted back and forth, while he licked his lips. "I was too sick to report this morning, sir."

"That's no excuse. If you're sick, you report for sick call."

"I—I was too sick to get up, sir."

Maurice rose and scowled. "The punishment for missing roll call is standing on the block for two hours."

The private cringed. "Sir, I'm too sick to stand for that long."

"Well—" Maurice studied his fingernails. "—I fear you shall have to endure it. If you pass out before your two hours are up, you'll start all over again once you come to."

The private's lips thinned. "Yes, sir," he ground out.

After he left, Maurice smiled. He truly knew how to treat those beneath him, and he enjoyed using the whip to deal with more serious offenses. Any enemies he encountered would meet a much more fearsome fate.

Chapter Eight

Cabin in northwestern Virginia
March 17, 1863

Alex woke the next day and glanced at the bed where Katie had slept, finding it empty. Rising, he moved to the door leading to the kitchen. He expected to find her scrounging up something for breakfast. The kitchen was empty. Where was she?

After the encounter yesterday, they'd avoided each other as best they could in the confines of the small cabin. He'd tended to the horses, and she'd busied herself in the kitchen. She refused to talk about her late husband, and he wouldn't admit how hurt he'd felt after she'd called him by her husband's name. When he'd kissed her, he hoped she truly wanted him.

At the sound of the door opening, he looked up. Katie entered lugging a bucket of water. She wore her gray army sack coat over the wrapper and apron.

"You should have awakened me," he said. "I would've fetched the water."

She dropped her gaze and shrugged. "I didn't want to disturb yer sleep."

He reached for the bucket and placed it on the hearth.

"There's not much left to eat, I fear." Abruptly, she turned away and busied herself preparing a mixture of oatmeal.

Returning to the other room, he poked at the logs in the fireplace. Maybe after they sat down to eat, he could broach the subject of what happened last night. If she hadn't responded as she had, he never would have gone as far as he did.

After a bit of time had passed with the sounds of clanging pots and then plates being set out, he decided to swallow his shame and help her. He stopped at the kitchen doorway and found she had everything under control.

She had tea steeping in a large pot on the table. "Mr. Hart, you may serve yourself while I dish out the porridge." She turned back to her task, but he'd noted the coldness in her eyes. And she was back to calling him *Mr. Hart*.

He took a seat at the table, poured himself a cup of tea, then filled her cup. He scraped a small amount of sugar into his spoon, making sure he left enough for her.

She approached with a steaming bowl and placed it in front of him. Taking her bowl, she returned to the hearth.

Once she'd sat across from him, Alex cleared his throat. "I want to apologize for my behavior yesterday."

She shrugged. "'Tis no need. I've all but forgotten the matter."

Alex's bile rose. How could she dismiss what happened between them so easily? The feel of her soft skin and lips against his naked flesh would be etched forever in his memory. He took a mouthful of tea to prevent himself from speaking. If that were the way she wanted it, he'd be happy to oblige.

****

Katie tried to keep her tone even. She couldn't allow the man to know how much his touch and the feel of his body had affected her. In a few days, they'd be leaving and would go their separate ways. She wasn't about to engage in sinful behavior with a man she'd likely never see again.

They finished eating in strained silence. She

was relieved when he shrugged into his coat to tend to the horses.

"After I'm done," he said, "I'll see if the snow's melted any."

She nodded, not holding out much hope. What they needed was a major warm up. The sun had risen an hour before, and she'd noted a hint of warmer air when she'd gone out for water, but they needed a miracle. They couldn't hold out in this tiny cottage much longer.

After cleaning up, Katie rifled through her haversack and pulled out her housewife kit. Extracting a needle and thread, she repaired the seam on her army trousers. When they left here, she intended to leave the dresses where she'd found them and return to her army clothing. Although she liked the freedom her male attire offered her, she had enjoyed wearing gowns again. She'd forgotten how it felt to have admiring male eyes on her.

Before she'd completed her task, Alex returned, took off his hat, and shrugged out of his coat. "If the weather keeps up like this, I believe we may be able to leave tomorrow."

"That's wonderful," Katie said.

He nodded, then went into the kitchen.

She knew she'd stirred lustful feelings in him yesterday, but Saints be praised, he was a gentleman. Otherwise, he would have ravaged her by now.

Knowing he was just in the other room, she found it hard to resist going to him. Everything about him, his smile, his laugh, his intense gaze as he watched her, his musky scent and especially his touch, sent a shiver through her. God help her, she wanted him.

But after tomorrow, they'd go their separate ways.

The next morning, Katie dressed in her army

uniform.

After eating and cleaning up, Alex left to prepare the horses. She tidied up the cottage and folded the dresses and underthings she'd worn.

She lifted one of the aprons and a paper fluttered out. She recognized the letter she'd found in Alex's pack. Hastily, she slid the note into her bag. She counted herself lucky he hadn't realized the letter was missing.

****

Alex saddled the horses in preparation for their departure. Snow still covered the ground but had now melted enough so they could navigate through. Last night he'd barely slept knowing Katie lay on the bed across from him. He'd longed to go to her and lie by her side, knowing this would be their last night together.

But he'd respected her wishes and stayed away.

He strapped on Rusty's bridle. His booted foot hit against something hard. He'd forgotten about the mailbag he'd stolen. He couldn't tell her the truth now. He could never tell her his reason for taking the satchel. If she discovered he was a Federal spy...

After eyeing his pack, he moved the contents of the mailbag into his and buried her bag in the rear of the stable. Now, he just needed to keep her out of his pack for the duration of the trip.

When she did join him, she wore trousers, her butternut sack coat and a gray kepi over her flame-red curls.

She expertly mounted her mare, then looked down at him. "Shall we be on our way then, Mr. Hart?"

He nodded. "Yes, ma'am." He climbed onto Rusty, stung by her coldness. But her sour mood had been his fault. He should have restrained himself and couldn't blame her.

After making their way slowly up the bank and

over the crusty slush to the road, they continued in silence. As the hours ran on, Alex rethought his plan about parting before she'd returned safely to camp. Since she'd lost her pistol in the stream, she was defenseless. How could he leave her to travel alone unarmed?

He was a Southerner in civilian garb riding with a Confederate soldier, so had nothing to fear from the Rebels. A Yankee patrol, however, could be a stickier situation.

He didn't have to make a decision yet. He'd wait until they'd gotten farther along to decide whether to separate and head south to Washington.

Stopping once, they ate the dried food they carried in their haversacks. After that, they continued on.

Except for polite conversation, they hardly spoke. Late afternoon, Alex reined in his gelding. "It's time we start looking for a place to spend the night, ma'am."

Katie glanced around. "We could stay the night out here a wee bit back from the road."

He nodded. "Reckon we'll ride a bit farther before we decide."

Minutes later, a fence and the scent of wood smoke signaled they'd arrived at the outskirts of a farm.

****

Katie had felt uneasy all day. She kept silent, unable to decide if she wanted to part from Alex. She knew he intended to travel south to Richmond. She could sense his hesitation, too, as if he wanted to speak but held back.

When they came upon the fence, he suggested they should stop for the night.

Circling around the barn, they tried to find someone they could ask for permission. No one was there, but they found a few cows, horses, and pigs settled in for the night. Smoke rose from the chimney of the farmhouse.

"Someone's home," Alex said. "Let's see if they'll let us bed down in the barn."

They approached the house. A male voice rang out.

"You there. Halt or I'll shoot!"

Katie halted Morna and glanced at Alex. He raised his hands in the air. She followed his lead, scanning for the source of the voice.

A blast startled her. Alex cried out and fell from his gelding.

Katie gasped. She feared she was the next target. "Don't shoot," Katie yelled. She lifted her hands above her head. "I'm a Confederate soldier."

She wanted to go to Alex, who lay writhing on the ground, but didn't dare move. She hoped these people weren't Federalists.

A young man with light brown hair rounded on her holding a shotgun. An older, gray-haired man raced from the house.

"*Was ist das!*" the older man demanded in a guttural accent.

Having no idea what the man was saying, Katie pointed at Alex. "He's been shot. I have to help him."

The young man said something in what sounded like German to the older man, who shook his head.

"I'm very sorry," he said, motioning to Katie. "Please, get down and see to your friend."

She slid from her mare and knelt at Alex's side. Fear chilled her to the bone, and she labored to draw a breath. "Are you hurt bad?"

He grimaced, clutching his thigh. "The son-of-a-bitch shot me." Blood oozed from a blackened tear in his trousers.

She went to her saddlebags and found a neckerchief. She tied it around his wound.

She glanced up at the farmer. "He needs help."

"Of course." The man nodded. To the young man beside him, he said, "Dieter, get your brother. We have to carry him into the house."

Dieter nodded, wide-eyed, and raced off.

"I must apologize for my son," the older man said. "Federal soldiers came through here two days ago and threatened us, then made off with some of our animals."

Katie's fists clenched. "I know what bastards Yankees can be."

The man's face relaxed. While they waited for his sons, he introduced himself. "My name is Arnold Bauer. I own this farm."

Katie nodded. "Private Sean O'Reilly of the 2nd Virginia. This is Mr. Alexander Hart. He's a newspaperman from Richmond."

"Please forgive Dieter," Bauer pleaded, appealing to Alex. "He was too hasty. He's afraid."

Katie glanced at Alex, who nodded. His face paled by the minute. What if the wound was fatal? She took a deep breath, trying to calm her fear.

"Ah, here they are," Bauer said as Dieter and another, strapping, blond-haired lad approached. This one was younger, but well-proportioned.

"Franz," Bauer said. "Help us get Mr. Hart into the house so your Momma can see to him."

Between the three of them, they lifted Alex and carried him toward the house while Katie led the horses to the barn.

****

Pain jerked Alex back to consciousness. His thigh hurt like hell. Opening his eyes, he tried to figure out where he was.

He moved his leg, and a sharp stab of pain brought everything back into focus. He remembered the farmhouse, the shot, falling from Rusty's back.

When the farmer and his sons had lifted him, he'd blacked out. How long had he been asleep, and where was Katie?

"Ach, you're awake." A buxom woman with brown hair streaked with gray approached him.

"Where am I?" he asked.

"The Bauer farm. I'm Mrs. Bauer and this—" She motioned behind her to a young, blond woman. "—is my daughter, Claudia."

The young woman's smile wavered.

"We've been seeing to your wound," Mrs. Bauer went on, "since the doctor left."

"Doctor?"

"Ya." She shook her head. "We could not wake you. My husband summoned Doc Hirsh. He treated your leg and told us how to care for you."

"Much obliged, ma'am," Alex said. "But could you tell me what became of the young lady traveling with me?"

The women exchanged puzzled glances.

"Lady?" Mrs. Bauer asked. "We saw no lady. You were with a young man. A soldier."

"Yes." Realizing Katie had reverted to her male identity, he corrected his mistake. "Pardon me, ma'am. I'm not quite myself yet. I must have been dreaming I was with a lady instead of a young man. Where is he?"

"Tending to your horses in the barn and helping my sons with the chores. He should be up to see you directly. Until then you must rest, unless we can get you anything."

"No, ma'am. I'll be just fine."

He dozed for what seemed only minutes when a familiar voice startled him awake.

"He still looks so pale," he heard Katie say.

"The doctor told Momma he'll be fine," a female voice assured her.

He opened his eyes to see Katie and Claudia standing over him. Katie's brows knitted together, but she smiled when he looked up at her.

"Could we be alone for a wee bit?" Katie asked Claudia.

"Of course." Claudia smiled at Alex. "Call me if you need anything."

After she left, he looked at Katie. Relief flooded through him knowing she was all right. He didn't want to imagine losing her.

"I take it you're still in male disguise," he said.

"Aye," she said. "'Tis easier to explain this way. And they don't seem to be any the wiser."

He rubbed a hand over his beard. "How long have I been out?"

"Most of the night."

"That long." He was alarmed at the passage of time. "The horses—"

"Are fine. I've been tending to them."

He tried to sit up, but groaned when a wave of pain hit his body. "Did this doctor say how long before I can ride?"

She glanced away for a moment, then gazed squarely at him. "He said a few weeks."

"Weeks?"

"You need time to heal and get yer strength back. You lost a great deal of blood."

He settled back against the headboard, sighing.

"I need to be getting back," he said.

"To Richmond?"

He nodded.

"'Tis one-hundred and fifty miles. Ye'll never make it with a wound like that."

He looked away. He had to get to Washington but couldn't tell her that. And right now, Washington seemed unattainable. "Reckon I'll have to stay like the doc ordered, but I'm sure you'll be moving on without me."

She bit her lip, drawing his gaze to her mouth. The memory of her sweet lips pressed against his, sent his pulse racing. "I thought I'd stay. At least for a few days."

Although she didn't fit in with his plans, he was glad to hear she wasn't leaving right away. He'd miss her when she left. But another thought crossed his mind. His saddlebag stuffed with Confederate mail.

He cleared his throat. "Where are my saddlebags?"

"In the barn with the horses. Do you need something from yer bag? I'll be only too glad to get it fer you."

"No, that won't be necessary. Just worried about my personal things."

She nodded. "I'll have the Bauer boys bring yer bags up here."

"That'll be fine. Thank you." He just hoped she wouldn't handle or look into the bags herself. She'd likely drag him to the Rebel camp to turn him in. If she didn't shoot him first.

****

As Alex slowly recovered over the next few weeks, he was able to get out of bed and move about the room. He'd sit watching from the window to catch a glimpse of Katie as she did chores alongside the Bauer boys.

Mrs. Bauer and Claudia brought his food and attended to his wound as the doctor had ordered, but Katie's visits were less frequent. Although she hadn't yet left, she seemed to be avoiding him.

One day, as he sat at the window, his leg propped on a stool, a light knock sounded at the door.

"Come in," he said.

Claudia strode in carrying a tray heaped with a basin, rags, and a fresh roll of bandages. After setting the tray on his bedside table, she went back to the open door and drew it shut.

Alex frowned. "I think it might be wise if you left

that open."

Claudia smiled. "I wouldn't worry about that, *Herr* Hart. Or may I call you Alex?"

"Uh...I don't think—"

"Mama, Papa, and my brothers are out in the field working. We won't be interrupted for a while, Alex."

Alex shifted, an uncomfortable knot forming in his stomach. "Miss Bauer—"

"Claudia."

Alex's mouth gaped as he tried to think of something to say.

"Please," Claudia said, "allow me to clean your wound. If you would lie down on the bed, it would make things much easier."

"Um...I don't..." Alex swallowed. "All right." He maneuvered himself with Claudia's assistance to the bed.

"Slide down your trousers, please." Claudia batted her eyes and bit her lip.

"I don't think we should be doing this with the door closed." Alex glanced at the door certain her father would burst in on them any minute and cause more damage then his son did with the gun.

"Nonsense. They are all outside. Now, lower your braces and loosen your trousers."

Alex swallowed, not liking this situation at all. But the faster they got this done, the faster she'd be out of here. He lowered his braces, unbuttoned his pants and slid them down low enough to expose the wound on his upper thigh just beneath the hem of his drawers. Fortunately, his shirt tail ballooned out over his private area.

A blush crept over Claudia's face as she gazed at his exposed thigh. "You must remove the trousers, so I can treat your wound."

Alex frowned, then lowered one pant leg over his knee, struggling to extract the injured leg from it.

Claudia tilted her head, biting her lip. "Both legs."

"Ma'am, this is the only leg you have to treat. I'm not about to get half-naked in front of a lady."

"But...?" Claudia sputtered.

"Are you sure your mama wasn't supposed to do this?" Alex asked.

"*Nein.*" Claudia lifted the scissors and cut the old bandage, exposing the wound. "*Ya,* it's looking much better." She raised her gaze to his. "Once the stitches are out, the scar will be small, not much to mar your fine skin."

Claudia licked her lips, as she sponged the area. Warm water against the stitches felt heavenly, but Alex tried not to show his pleasure. He avoided watching Claudia, allowing his gaze to flit around the room.

As Claudia dried the wound, Alex had a hard time suppressing his reaction to her soft, feathery touch.

Claudia wrapped a fresh bandage around his thigh. "Your muscles are well developed. I can tell you're used to hard work."

A knock at the door, followed by the knob turning, startled Alex.

Katie stood in the doorway, arms crossed, and a scowl creasing her face.

****

Katie glared at Claudia. "May I have a word with Mr. Hart, please?"

Claudia gathered her things, a smirk on her face. She leveled a glare at Katie, then glanced back at Alex.

"I'll be by later, Alex."

She brushed past Katie and headed down the stairs.

Katie rounded on Alex, still lying on the bed. "And what, may I ask, was that all about?"

Alex waved his hand. "She was cleaning and dressing my wound." He grimaced as he bent his bandaged leg trying to push it back into his trousers.

"Was she now? With the door shut? Yer half-naked!" Katie felt as if steam would push out of her ears.

"That's all there was to it, I swear." Alex yanked up his trousers, buttoned them, and pushed himself into a seated position against the pillows.

"The girl's set her cap for you." Katie planted her hands on her hips.

"So what if she has? I for sure haven't encouraged her. In fact, I've done everything in my power to *discourage* her."

"She didn't look discouraged to me. And why is she calling you Alex?"

He shrugged as he adjusted his braces. "I never invited her to call me by my first name."

Images of Alex and Claudia raced through Katie's mind. How had she been so stupid? He'd never cared for her. He'd only wanted to take advantage of her back at the cabin.

"Good day, Mr. Hart." Katie strode from the room, slammed the door, and stood at the railing, seething. She should have left weeks ago.

She stormed down the stairs and out the door.

****

Surprisingly, Katie hadn't left. Although she'd been furious when she'd found Claudia flirting with him, she'd stayed on helping the boys with their chores. She only visited his sickroom occasionally, and he hadn't had the opportunity to make amends. He wanted her to understand that Claudia meant nothing to him. She was just a pretty face, nothing more.

When Katie was around him, he didn't see the gangly boy the others saw, he saw a lovely woman who he longed to kiss and much more. But he had to support her wishes to be taken for a male. So, although he longed to show her how he felt and feel her in his arms again, he kept his peace.

Having to pretend she was male proved pure torture. Whenever she laughed or smiled, the memory of her sweet kisses, threatened to cause him to compromise her disguise. But he wouldn't do that in front of the Bauers.

And, as far as he could see, her disguise was working. No one in the family had caught on.

A week later, Alex approached the Bauer's barn. Only a few puffy clouds dotted the blue sky on this clear and warm, early April day. His leg had healed, leaving only a pink scar and some annoying stiffness. And Mrs. Bauer's hearty German cooking had brought back his strength. During the past week, he'd relied on a cane, but with the pain lessening, he could walk on his own and was ready to move on.

He entered the barn to check on Rusty and found Katie seated on a pile of hay surrounded by a litter of kittens and the two youngest Bauer children, Greta and Peter.

"...and the Leprechaun said to him, 'Ye'll never find me pot of gold.'"

Greta clapped her hands and shook her head, sending her chestnut braids bobbing over her shoulders. "And then what happened?"

"Why, he tried to force the Leprechaun to tell him where his gold was hidden." Katie glanced up at Alex. "Yer looking well."

He shrugged. "Thank you. I'm getting my strength back."

"Go play with the kittens," Katie urged the children. "I'll be needing to have a word with Mr. Hart."

The children scrambled after the squirming animals. Katie rose, escorting him to Rusty's stall.

"I take it ye'll be leaving, then." She held his gaze.

"Yes. I assume you're coming with me."

"Aye. As far as Berryville." She looked away, and the pain of leaving her hit him in the gut.

"Look. I know what you think about Claudia, but I have no feelings for her."

"I know what I saw." Katie lowered her gaze.

"No, you don't." He lifted her chin, forcing her gaze to meet his. "If you weren't disguised as a male, I'd show you right now just how much you mean to me."

She stared hard at him. Then lowered her head. "I don't know how I feel right now."

His breath hitched. He couldn't allow this to remain between them. "I mean it, Katie," he said quietly. "You're the only woman I care about."

She took a deep breath, then nodded. "Aye, I believe you."

Alex smiled. "Thank you. And my plans are to accompany you back to your regiment. They're in Berryville?"

"Near enough. At least, I hope they're still there. I've been sidetracked for a long time."

"I'll accompany you that far," he said. "It's the least I can do, since I caused you to lose your sidearm."

"'Tis me own fault. I was clumsy."

He shook his head. "You forget, I've seen you ride. You're nowhere near clumsy. You're a skilled and graceful horsewoman. I take it you rode before joining the army."

Glancing at the children, she motioned him to silence, but they seemed too occupied with the kittens to notice the adults' conversation.

"Aye. Rory taught me to ride after we married." She gestured toward the stall that held her mare. "Morna is the foal of the horse I first learned to ride.

The Yankees took her from me."

Alex glanced back at the tumbling children. "You have a way with children. Someday you'll have a whole brood of babies, I'm sure."

He wasn't prepared for the look of pain that crossed her features.

"I don't know about that, Mr. Hart."

Chapter Nine

Two weeks later, Alex strapped on Rusty's bridle. He'd already saddled the gelding and attached his bags. Katie did the same with Morna.

"'Tis two or three miles to Berryville." Katie settled onto her mare. "The camp should be just east of there. We can easily make it by nightfall." She searched his face. "You could stay the night before you head south."

He hesitated. What would he do about the Rebel mail? He didn't want to be caught with it in his possession, especially at an enemy camp. And if she found it—that might be worse than dealing with a whole company of Rebel soldiers. But leaving it here with the Bauers wasn't an option either. He had no choice but to take it along.

"Sounds like a plan." Alex hoped his unease didn't sound in his voice.

They said their goodbyes to the Bauer family. Katie bid farewell to each of the children in turn. She whispered something to the two youngest that made them giggle.

Despite the unhappiness on her face, Claudia focused doe-eyes on him that he did his best to ignore. He glimpsed at Katie to make sure she hadn't seen Claudia's reaction. Spending time alone with Katie would feel good, even if they *were* destined to spend the night in a Rebel camp.

Lord help him. Maybe he could turn the stay to his advantage. By keeping his eyes and ears open, he could gather more timely information to report to Washington than what could be gleaned from the month-old mail. But first, he'd have to get rid of the pouch at the first opportunity.

Alex noticed spring buds that had recently opened to colorful blossoms graced the trees, and wildflowers lay sprawled along the edge of the road. When they stopped to rest, a wild rosebush bearing pale pink blossoms caught Alex's eye. He plucked one and presented it to Katie.

She held the rose under her nose and smiled. "A lass could get used to treatment like this."

He smiled. "You're a lady. And it's high time you were treated like one."

"Me da used to call me Katie Rose."

"Katie Rose? I like that."

"'Tis one of me middle names. It was also me ma's name. Da used to call us his rose garden."

Alex smiled. "*One* of your middle names? How many do you have?"

"Me full name is Kathryn Rose Margaret Mary Coyne O'Reilly."

"A good Irish name," Alex agreed. "I may just start calling you Katie Rose."

Her face fell. "Once we're back in camp, we've got to be careful. No one can know I'm a woman."

"None of the men suspect?" Although he'd been fooled at first, he couldn't imagine her living day to day with men who didn't have a clue.

She shook her head. "No one but Patrick knows."

"Patrick?"

"Me brother-in-law."

"That's right. You told me about him."

"Everyone else thinks I'm his younger brother, Sean."

Worried for her safety, he asked, "Are you sure you want to go back to that life?"

"'Tis the only life I have now. I won't go back to me family in New York City."

"I take it things were bad there."

She grimaced. "Worked twelve hours a day in a dark, dingy yarn factory, I did. Each night, I came home exhausted, to a filthy tenement where I had to help me ma cook for me da and brothers and clean up after them."

"Sounds like a hard life," he admitted. "But the army can't be easy either. And you have to pretend to be someone you're not."

"'Tis simple enough. The other men see a boy. As long as I wear men's clothing, none of them are any the wiser."

Alex shook his head. "I see you as a beautiful woman, despite the clothes."

Katie blushed a bright pink. "That's because you know. Ye've seen me as I am and can't get the image from yer mind. Rory never forgot."

Alex cleared his throat. "We'd best get moving if we want to make camp by nightfall." In truth, he wanted to get to the camp to ease his temptation. He longed to take her in his arms and remove her clothing, one piece at a time. He'd kiss her bare flesh, starting with her rosebud lips and continue until he sampled all of her.

He'd already seen her naked in her sickbed, but now she was robust and healthy. If they stayed here any longer, he'd be unable to resist his impulses.

****

The sun had dipped below the horizon, when Katie led Alex into the camp of her Virginia regiment.

"Sean," one of the pickets said, "good to see you back."

"Glad to be back, Grady."

The big, blond-haired man looked from her to Alex. His gaze narrowed suspiciously. "And who's this?"

"A friend," Katie said. "Private Grady, meet Mr. Hart. He's a newspaperman from Richmond."

Grady stared at Alex. "Whoo-wee! You write stories for the paper?"

"Reckon so," Alex said.

"Could you write a story about me, newspaper man?"

"Later," Katie told him. "We have to tend to our horses."

"Go right ahead." Grady waved them into camp. "Your brother will be relieved to see you alive and well."

She sent Alex a warning glance. They continued into the camp. Once out of the picket's earshot, she said, "Patrick has been overly protective of me since Rory was killed."

Alex's face hardened, and she wondered if he'd consider Patrick a rival. "He treats me as he would his sister," she assured him.

He nodded, but his frown deepened.

After leaving their horses to be tended to by one of the soldiers, Katie led Alex to her tent, to leave her things.

"Sean!" a strident, male voice called.

She turned to look into Patrick's hazel eyes. Hatless, his dark rust-red hair stood out in disarray.

"Where have you been all this time? I feared the Yankees had shot you or captured you and sent you to one of their godawful prisons." He stroked his beard while his sharp gaze went from her to Alex.

"This is Mr. Hart," she answered the question in Patrick's eyes. "He saved me life."

The two men eyed each other warily. Patrick reached out hesitantly to shake Alex's hand. "And how did you accomplish this great feat, sir?"

Alex shook his head. "It was really nothing."

"First, he saved me from drowning, then nursed me through a fever that surely would've taken me life," Katie said.

Patrick's eyes widened.

"He knows," she whispered.

Patrick nodded. "Then I'm eternally grateful to you, sir. She's all I have."

Standing between the two men, Katie got the feeling they were not destined to be the best of friends. "Mr. Hart's a newspaperman from Richmond." To Alex, she said, "This is Sergeant Patrick O'Reilly, me brother-in-law.

"He'll stay the night before moving on," she explained. "Can we find a spare tent for him?"

Patrick nodded, still watching Alex warily. "He can bunk in me tent. I've got picket duty half the night."

"Thank you, sir," Alex said. "That will be fine."

"All right then," Katie said. "Now that's settled, I'll show Alex to your tent where he can leave his things."

"Alex?" Patrick's gaze narrowed.

"Er..." Katie stammered. "Mr. Hart."

She led Alex off but didn't miss the withering stare Patrick threw her way, as well as the satisfied smile on Alex's face.

****

As a matter of course, Alex was escorted and introduced to the commanding officer, Colonel Wiggins. The dark-haired colonel was accommodating, ushering Alex to a seat in his tent while his aide prepared a pass so Alex could have free reign of the camp.

"From Richmond, you say?" The colonel offered Alex a cup of coffee.

"Yes, sir," Alex answered before lifting the mug to take a sip.

Wiggins studied the pass the aide handed him. "Alex Hart. Well, sir, I'll be sure to be on the lookout for your byline. My family lives in Richmond."

Alex cleared his throat. "I'll be sure to include your name, sir, in my articles." Of course, he planned to be long gone by the time the colonel realized Alex wasn't on staff at the paper. Alex spent the remainder of the day moving through camp conversing with soldiers. When they learned he worked for a Richmond newspaper, they were all the more eager to supply information.

"Heard we're movin' south some, sir," a dark-haired, young man told him.

"Do you know whereabout?" Alex asked.

"I heard troops are buildin' around Chancellorsville," a brown haired corporal piped in. "That's where we's going, I reckon."

"Chancellorsville," Alex repeated.

"Maybe you'd best head thataway," the younger soldier suggested.

"Maybe I will," Alex said.

He spent the rest of the evening questioning soldiers, and then exhausted, crawled into O'Reilly's tent to get some sleep. He closed his eyes, but his mind still churned. Maybe it was time to switch disguises. If the Rebels were heading to Chancellorsville, he could find a way to stay with them and travel right into the thick of things.

****

The next morning, while Katie stood with the men for roll call, she caught sight of Alex talking to the colonel.

Knowing he planned to leave today sent her stomach tumbling. She didn't want him to go, although she knew he had important business in Richmond. Once he left, she feared she'd never see him again.

After the troops were dismissed, she followed the others to the mess tent. An older man with blond-gray hair and beard dispensed eggs and slabs of bacon. While she waited her turn, tin plate in her hands, she sensed a presence behind her. She turned and looked into Alex's eyes.

"Gettin' yerself breakfast before you leave?" she asked.

He smiled. "I won't be leaving. At least not right away."

"But I thought you'd pressing business down in Richmond. The paper..."

"I resigned," he said.

"You what?"

"I decided I'd be more help carrying a rifle than a notepad. I spoke to the colonel and signed up. Call me Private Hart of the 2nd Virginia."

Goosebumps rose up Katie's arms. "Then you'll serve in this company?"

He nodded. "I can't leave now if I want to."

As much as she longed for him to stay, she'd never expected this turn of events. What was behind his change of plans? Could there be more to his story than what he's revealing. Maybe he hid his real motive.

Chapter Ten

Alex wasn't sure Katie quite trusted him. But she'd brought him to this camp, and he'd given her no solid reason to suspect him of anything. Especially since he'd disposed of the Rebel correspondence by sending the bag down stream. He'd dumped it when she thought he'd gone to relieve himself on the last stop before they made camp. He had nothing on him, except...the dispatch. How could he have forgotten that? The letter was still in his pack. Could be a fiery red-head had distracted him. He'd have to read and burn it first chance he got.

Joining the Rebel army would give him the perfect opportunity to gather information. Soldiers said things to each other they'd never say to a newspaperman. Plus, he'd be privy to orders sooner.

Later that afternoon, Alex engaged a few soldiers in conversation to gather more information. From the corner of his eye, he caught sight of Katie approaching. He had to be on his guard since most of the men knew her as *Sean*.

She smiled then joined the men in the discussion of where they would be sent.

"We're moving south, then?" Katie said.

A wiry, gray-haired soldier nodded. "Goin' to meet the Yankees at Chancellorsville is what I heard."

Alex remained silent but absorbed all that was said. Chancellorsville would take him a bit closer to Washington, but not by all that much. He'd have to find a way to smuggle messages out if he wanted to

86

stay under cover and not be charged with desertion by the Rebels.

Since Katie knew him as Alex Hart, he'd signed up using his real name. He didn't think it would present a problem, though. If they checked on him, and he doubted they would, they'd find he was a resident of Richmond, Virginia, and the son of a plantation owner.

If my father could see me now. But his family's rejection brought him to this point. They'd disowned him when he refused to fight for the Confederacy. Annabelle had slapped his face and ended their engagement. She claimed he'd dishonored both her and his family.

He was completely on his own. No ties, except to his friend, Elliot James, who he'd lived with in Pennsylvania while attending a university before the war. Elliot was a surgeon with the Union Army and the only family Alex now had.

He wondered what Katie would do if she found out he was a Federal spy. Would she slap his face like Annabelle had or spear him with her bayonet? Knowing her demeanor, he'd bet on the bayonet.

Once the others drifted away, Katie moved closer and whispered, "I'm proud of what ye've done. I'll be honored to stand beside you in battle."

Her sweet, musky scent caused his senses to reel, and he felt himself grow hard. He longed to lean over and take her mouth. A male voice stopped him from doing just that.

"There you are, Sean, me boy-o." Patrick strode up to them. He glanced at Alex. "Saw yer name on the picket roster. Looks as though ye'll be on duty with me tonight."

"So I am, Sergeant," Alex said.

Katie smiled. "I'll be seeing you tomorrow, then."

"I look forward to it."

Alex watched Katie move toward her tent but

felt Patrick's eyes on him.

The Irishman rounded on him, blocking his view. "I'll be seeing you on picket, Hart."

Alex nodded and wondered what Patrick would have to say to him once they were alone. The man's feelings for Katie went much deeper than those for a sister.

****

Alex held the butt of his Enfield rifle propped under his armpit. The overcast sky made it difficult to see but a few feet in front of him. Patrick was stationed a few yards away to his left. As a new recruit, Alex had been issued a cap and rifle, but his civilian clothing had to suffice for a uniform, since there were none to be had this late in the war. Half the Confederate Army now wore blue, Union trousers.

Patrick said little when Alex reported for picket duty, but the Irishman appeared wary of Alex.

After a half hour, Patrick moved a bit closer. "Are you all right?" he called.

"Just fine and dandy, Sergeant," Alex replied.

"I thought with all yer travels ye'd be dead on yer feet."

"Must have gotten a second wind."

Patrick closed the gap between them. "I was just wonderin'..." He stopped.

"About me and your sister-in-law?" Alex guessed.

Patrick nodded. "She said you saved her life twice. She's young and impressionable, and me brother's only been in the grave six months."

"You want to know if I've taken advantage of her."

"Aye."

"And if I have, you'll likely shoot me." Alex inclined his head toward Patrick's rifle.

"I just might that," the sergeant replied.

"Allow me to assure you, though I'm tempted, I respect Katie. I would never do anything without her consent."

"And did she give you that, now?" Patrick glowered.

"No, sir, she didn't."

Patrick nodded, appearing satisfied.

Alex had been given a respite for now but knew the sergeant would be keeping an eye on him.

****

Confederate camp south of
Chancellorsville, Virginia
April 13, 1863

Alex grew used to the routine of army life. This wasn't at all new, since he'd spent the early part of the war as a Union soldier. Once recruited as a spy, he'd advanced to the rank of captain, and a year had passed since he'd been in the rank and file.

When on a mission, he traveled alone. To obtain information, he disguised himself in diverse occupations—a local farmer, reporter, clergyman, a bereaved relative searching for his soldier brother's body...whatever fit the situation. This was the first time he'd taken on the guise of an enemy soldier. As a Southerner, though, he fit in well enough. He'd learned to live by his wits. Now he had to learn to follow orders, at least to outward appearances. He wouldn't have as much freedom to move about but could gain more information from the inside.

He was a bit worried, though, about the dispatch. He'd searched his pack, but it wasn't there. He should have opened it weeks ago but had forgotten. He was definitely slipping in his diligence. He now had no clue as to his orders, and if someone else had found it, he could be in a heap of trouble.

The scent of wood smoke from cooking fires tinged the air. Alex wove his way through rows of tents, hoping to spot Katie. The drawl of a familiar female voice froze him.

It can't be!

He glanced behind him and quickly pulled the brim of his cap down to shield his face. A well-dressed woman with wheat-colored curls escaping the brim of her bonnet watched him.

"Soldier," she called, her voice sugary as syrup. "Where can I find Captain Bernard?"

"Sorry, ma'am," he muttered. He desperately hoped she wouldn't recognize him. "I'm new here. I don't know the captain."

He kept his face averted and breathed a sigh of relief when she abruptly spun in the other direction, calling after another soldier while her hooped skirt swirled out behind her.

Damnation! Of all the bad luck. He'd heard Annabelle had gotten engaged again to a Confederate officer. Damned if the man was stationed in this camp.

If she recognized him, he'd have to explain what he was doing here. Of course, she and his family had no idea he spied for the Yankees. When he'd left to go north, he'd cut off all ties.

Alex's curiosity piqued. Who had Annabelle chosen as a replacement? Not that he'd want her back. She no longer wanted the same things, if she ever had.

He had to know who the man was, though, if only to steer clear.

Moving from tree to tree, Alex concealed himself and followed Annabelle. A corporal pointed her in the direction of a tarp set before a large wall-tent where several officers sat in conversation.

When she approached the men, an auburn-haired officer with a thick, handlebar mustache rose and took her gloved hand.

Alex hugged a wide oak, so they wouldn't catch him watching and tried to follow the conversation.

"Maurice," Annabelle cooed. "I've missed you so."

He kissed her fingers. "While I'm delighted to see you, darlin', I'd rather you not travel so far. It's dangerous."

"Oh." She pouted. "You sound like Papa."

"I do hope he escorted you."

"Yes, of course. But he returned to town on some business-or-other. He'll be by later to escort me back to Winchester."

"Very well," the captain said, "I'll give you a tour of the camp."

When she grasped his arm, Alex turned away.

Maybe it was for the best she'd jilted him. Being married to a woman like that would be a trial.

Alex lifted his kepi and ran his fingers through his hair. A messenger passed by and approached the captain. Annabelle moved aside, while Bernard attended to a note. She looked in Alex's direction. Hoping she hadn't noticed him watching, Alex stuffed his hands into his pockets and ambled away. So long as she didn't see him and made her visits infrequent, he should be able to keep his identity from the captain.

Annabelle's drawl stopped him. "Soldier, I believe I know you from somewhere."

Damnation! He half-turned toward her, keeping his gaze lowered.

"You look familiar," she said. "Have we met before?" Her sudden gasp set his teeth on edge. "Alex?"

He lifted his gaze to meet her startled blue eyes.

"I thought you'd returned north," she said. "What are you doing here?"

"I came to my senses." He took her arm, discreetly leading her away so Captain Bernard wouldn't hear.

"Why didn't you contact me? Or your family?" Her gaze narrowed as she looked him up and down.

91

He shrugged. "You'd jilted me, and my father disowned me. Why bother?"

"Why, I wouldn't have..." She lifted a hand to her mouth.

Alex folded his arms across his chest. "Wouldn't have accepted *his* proposal?"

"You left me no choice, Alex." She laid a gloved hand on the arm of his coat. "You should have told me. It would have changed things."

Alex sighed. "You made your choice, Annabelle. Best wishes for your impending union." He turned away, but she grasped his arm.

****

Maurice glanced up from the dispatch his aide had handed him. Where the devil had Annabelle gone? The last thing he wanted was her roaming unescorted through camp.

His gaze caught sight of her hoopskirt. She stood a few yards away behind a copse of trees conversing with a soldier. She leaned toward him, laying her hand on his sleeve. Her movements seemed intimate. Then as the soldier made to move away, she grasped his arm.

As Maurice watched, his blood heated. The man looked familiar. He was a recent recruit. *The reporter. What was his name?* Maurice tried to recall, but all thoughts deserted him as Annabelle stood on her toes and planted a kiss on the soldier's cheek.

The soldier turned and left. Annabelle stood gazing after him.

Maurice stared at her back, until she finally turned and found him watching her. She lifted her chin.

Well, well. Maurice folded his arms across his chest and watched her approach.

"Who was that?" he demanded.

Annabelle waved an arm. "An old friend of the family. I knew him as a child."

"I will not have you fraternizing with soldiers. You're my fiancée, not a harlot."

Annabelle gasped. "How dare you insult me!"

"If you act like a lady, you'll be treated as one. But if you dishonor me..." He grasped her arm and squeezed.

Her face colored. "You're hurting me, Maurice."

He released his hold on her. "Once your father returns, I *will* have a word with him about keeping you home to await my return."

Annabelle glared at him but didn't say a word. Perhaps she'd be easy to control, after all.

****

An hour later, Maurice heaved a sigh when Annabelle's father, Mr. Carswell, arrived to escort her back to town.

"Good afternoon, sir." Maurice grasped his future father-in-law's hand. "I've so enjoyed escorting Annabelle through camp."

Mr. Carswell beamed. "She insisted I bring her on this trip seeing as how close I would be to your regiment."

Swallowing a retort, Maurice said, "I'd prefer she sent letters and awaited visits from me at home."

"Well, son, you must know by now how stubborn our Annabelle can be."

"Papa," Annabelle said, "why must you speak about me as if I weren't here? It's my right to visit my fiancé whenever I wish." She twirled a finger in the ties of her bonnet and scowled at Maurice.

Is she challenging me? Maurice flushed and turned to Mr. Carswell. "I do trust, sir, you will be on your way home tomorrow."

Carswell nodded, while Annabelle frowned.

"Oh yes, of course," Carswell said. "We'll spend the night in Winchester and depart for Richmond first thing tomorrow."

Maurice escorted them to their carriage and gave Annabelle a chaste kiss while giving her arm a warning squeeze.

"You *will* be awaiting my return in Richmond." It wasn't a question.

"Yes, Maurice. Goodbye." She turned away and settled in the carriage.

Her father turned to shake Maurice's hand. "I quite understand your sentiments, son. I'll be sure she stays home. She and her mother will be occupied with wedding plans, no doubt."

"I do hope that will keep her out of trouble, sir."

"Yes. I'm sure it will."

Maurice watched their carriage crest the hill. What would his future with his fiancée be like? Although beautiful, Annabelle often infuriated him when she refused to take his orders seriously. But he still had been pleased to have been given her hand despite her pampered lifestyle. Unfortunately, her father overindulged her and gave in to her whims all too often. All that would change when they married. Once they recited their vows and she was under his roof, he'd whip her into submission. It worked on his father's slaves as well as disobedient recruits serving under him. He wouldn't hesitate to use it to tame a recalcitrant wife.

Chapter Eleven

Woods Outside Chancellorsville, Virginia
May 2,1863

Ducking behind a wide oak, Alex bit off the end of the round and tapped powder into the barrel of his Enfield. Raising his ramrod, he tamped the powder down. He glanced over his shoulder to be sure no one noticed he'd neglected to insert a bullet. Although he had to appear to participate in the coming battle, he'd be damned if he'd fire on Federal soldiers.

The Virginia regiment joined General Jackson's forces to the west of Chancellorsville. Federal forces stood between them and the town.

He planned to take advantage of the confusion that ensued once they'd drawn Federal fire and duck out, but Katie stuck to him like glue. He couldn't run off without her notice. He also had no desire to leave her side. If need be, he'd take a bullet to protect her.

He glanced to the other side of Katie where Patrick hovered. Now was not the time to aggravate the man further. The battle heated up. They steadily advanced on the Federal soldiers. Alex loaded and fired blanks while Katie fought like a demon. He couldn't help but admire her strength. She screamed her rage at the enemy, felling soldiers with her fire. That and her delicate beauty, though hidden, made him wish he could keep her by his side always.

****

Having Alex by her side comforted Katie— almost like the times with Rory. But Alex was nothing like her late husband. Although she'd loved

Rory for the good life he'd given her, he'd been rough and coarse. Alex was a Virginia gentleman, and she'd never been with such a refined man.

When the officers urged them into the horde of Yankees, Alex stayed by her side. Screaming, she fired at the enemy soldiers. In her mind she saw those men who'd raided the O'Reilly farm, killed her father-in-law, shot Patrick, and caused the death of her wee babe. Rory's son.

Her fury kept her loading and firing as her heart pounded. Beads of sweat formed on her brow. She wanted to kill them all for what they'd done to her.

She glanced at Alex and caught him pouring powder into his barrel, then tamp it down with his ramrod.

"You fergot yer bullet," she said.

"Oh, so I did." He grinned sheepishly and pulled a bullet from his pouch. She returned to her own loading.

****

Katie collapsed on the blanket spread over the bed of straw piled in her tent. She'd survived another battle. At times she believed Rory still watched over her and kept her from harm.

"Thank you, Rory," she whispered. Amorous feelings for Alex caused her to flush with guilt. Alex's warmth and presence beside her felt right.

Reaching for her pack, she extracted her flask. She'd filled it with whiskey but had left it behind when they'd gone into battle. She took a quick swig. The liquid burned down her throat. Warmth spread throughout her body, easing her shattered nerves. When she replaced the flask, her fingers brushed against a paper. She fished it out and recognized the letter she'd taken from Alex's pack. She'd never had the chance to read it. She licked her lips. She needed to know what was in the letter but at the same time, feared to know. What if it was a love letter to another woman?

She took a deep breath, broke the seal, and spread the paper. Her eyes widened in disbelief when she realized it was an official dispatch from Washington. They were orders for a Captain Alexander Hart of the Army of the Potomac.

Her chest tightened, and she found it hard to breathe. Alexander Hart? That's how he'd introduced himself the day they'd met. She tried to fathom why he'd have a Federal dispatch with his name on it. She tried to come to any conclusion other than the obvious. He was a Yankee, and he'd lied to her.

****

Alex settled before the fire, the stress of battle now behind him. He felt lucky to have survived. The Rebels declared the battle a victory, and the Union Army had retreated. But the Confederates lost General Jackson. He'd been accidentally shot by his own men the night before the battle.

Despite the Rebel victory, maybe the loss of Jackson would bode well for the Union.

Too keyed up to sleep, he took a swig from his flask. One of the other soldiers had given him a bit of Scotch. While it burned its way down his throat, he recalled the last battle where he'd been in the ranks.

He hadn't been engaged in combat since last September at Antietam. There he'd been with Federal troops. That had been a massacre for both sides. Since he'd become a spy, he usually witnessed battles from the sidelines.

This latest battle had taken a toll on him. He felt drained and needed to recoup and get some rest. Leaning back against a rock, he looked at the stars dotting the blackness. Moonlight brightened the landscape, producing an eerie glow.

Katie by his side in battle was also a new experience. Although he knew she was an experienced soldier and could hold her own, an overwhelming urge rose to protect her. A woman should be home tending to the hearth, waiting for her man to return from battle.

His thoughts drifted to Annabelle. Was she back in Richmond waiting for word of her new fiancé? Their brief encounter assured him he no longer had feelings for her, but he worried that she'd revealed his identity to her husband-to-be. Since the captain hadn't confronted him, though, he doubted she had.

Smoke from the fire drifted to him, stinging his eyes. He wiped his sleeve across his face. When he opened them, a soldier approached. He focused his vision and realized Katie strode toward him. She'd acquired a new slouch hat from her brother-in-law. The large, black hat concealed her red curls.

When she settled down cross-legged beside him, her mood seemed pensive. She watched him a moment before speaking.

"I found something that belongs to you."

His mouth went dry. Something was wrong. "What have you got?"

"I'm hating to have to say it, since I'd accused *you* of being a thief, but I stole something from you." She looked away.

"What could you...?" He racked his mind trying to figure out what she could have taken.

"I went through yer pack."

"In Patrick's tent?"

"No, weeks ago back at the cabin. I went through it to try to learn more about you when you were in the stable. I found a letter and took it but didn't have time to read it until now."

Alex swallowed.

"It was a Federal dispatch. Yer a Yankee."

His chest tightened. No wonder he'd been unable to find the dispatch. She'd had it all along. "What do you intend to do?" He hoped she wouldn't discover his real motive. He could never harm her.

"You lied to me the whole time," she said, disbelief marring her delicate features.

He exhaled the breath he'd held. "I had no choice."

"If I'd known you to be a Yankee, I'd have shot you the first chance I got." Her eyes glittered in the light of the fire. "You touched me...pretended to care fer me. And all the while, you lied to me."

The raw hurt on her face broke his heart. He'd deceived her. He couldn't deny it. "What do you intend to do?" he asked again.

She shook her head slowly. "I'm sorry, Alex, but 'tis me duty to turn you in."

****

Katie watched Alex's face pale. Had he really believed she'd forgive him?

"Katie, I know I've hurt you, but it was necessary. I'll get my things and leave...you'll never have to see me again."

"You bloody bastard!" She slapped his face, her hand stinging at the force of the blow. "Ye've taken everything from me." Heat rose in her cheeks at the indignity of what he'd done to her...he and his Yankee friends.

"I've lost everything because of Yankee devils...me home, me husband, and child."

He raised shocked eyes to her. "You never told me you had a child."

"A babe born dead because of what your soldiers did!" Her breathing grew ragged. She wanted to scream, but he would hear her out. "Me father-in-law was shot and killed by Union soldiers, trying to protect his farm and family. Me mother-in-law died shortly after from a broken heart. I was heavy with child at the time. Days later, I delivered a stillborn. A little boy. After our babe died, Rory and Patrick joined the army. I went with them because the farm was left in ruins. I had nowhere else to go and had lost as much as they. I fought at me husband's side until he was killed in battle at Sharpsburg."

She took a deep breath. "Me only purpose in life is to kill Yankees, and now I find yer one of them."

Alex bowed his head. "I'm so sorry. If I'd have known..."

"What?" she demanded. "Would you have taken pity on the poor Rebel soldier?"

"I would've left you be."

"'Tis too late fer that!"

****

Alex bowed his head while Katie stormed away. He should get up, get his things, and skedaddle out of here, but his limbs wouldn't obey. He'd lost what he wanted most. Without Katie he had no reason to go on. He no longer cared what happened to him.

He sat for what could only have been minutes, but seemed like hours. His memories drifted over every moment he'd spent with Katie. Their time together hadn't been nearly enough but would have to last him a lifetime...or as long as the Rebels would allow him to live.

She returned with Patrick on her heels. The Irish sergeant aimed his rifle at Alex, motioning for him to rise.

"He's a Yankee sent to spy on us, and I've got proof." Her beautiful eyes hardened, shooting daggers at him.

Alex stood and raised his arms. "I won't give you any trouble," he told Patrick.

When Patrick led him away, Alex clenched his jaw. If only he'd been able to tell Katie he loved her. But now it was too late.

****

Katie retreated to her tent and crawled inside. Her jaw and head ached. She'd held her tears until she achieved her revenge, but the feeling was hollow. Her eyes stung, and her mouth quivered. She collapsed across the blanket and broke into sobs.

How could he have done this to her? After he'd saved her life twice and taken care of her when she was ill; she'd come to trust him. She should have opened the letter back in the cabin, then she could have struck him down before he set her body aflame and stole her heart.

Oh, Rory, I'm so sorry. She'd betrayed her husband's memory. Thank the Lord she'd stopped Alex before she'd lain with him. Since that day, they hadn't had the opportunity.

Rory had watched over her and protected her virtue. But it hurt so. She despised herself for loving a vile Yankee liar.

Rory would forgive her, but could she ever forgive herself?

Chapter Twelve

One of the colonel's aides informed Maurice they had a suspected Yankee in the guardhouse and the prisoner, one of his new recruits, had possibly been sent to spy on them.

Before he questioned the prisoner, he'd asked for Sergeant O'Reilly—the man who'd apprehended the soldier—to relate the incident to him.

O'Reilly reported, and Maurice motioned for him to sit.

"Now, Sergeant," Maurice said. "How is it you came to discover this Yankee in our midst?"

"Me brother came upon a Federal dispatch with the man's name on it, sir."

"Your brother...?"

"Private Sean O'Reilly, sir."

"I see." Maurice sat back. "And what is this Yankee's name?"

"Captain Alexander Hart, sir."

Maurice frowned. Where had he heard that name before? He waved his hand. "Dismissed, Sergeant."

O'Reilly saluted and left.

Alexander Hart. I know that name. Scanning his memory, it suddenly came to him. Alexander Hart was the name of the plantation owner's son Annabelle had been engaged to before him—and the Richmond newspaperman, the one who'd recently joined the ranks had given his name as Alex Hart— he was also the one he'd seen speaking with Annabelle. They bore the same name and were obviously the same man. Maurice couldn't wait to question this prisoner.

****

Alex sagged on the hard bench in the dank guardhouse, his head in his hands. He couldn't deny the charges against him, since Katie had the dispatch. He didn't even care to.

His whole life was a lie. The day he'd left his father's home, in disgrace, he knew he could never go back.

Katie had made him feel whole again, but he'd lied to her. He'd broken her heart and his own, too.

Whatever the Rebels did to him, he'd accept gladly. His life no longer mattered.

After what seemed hours later, Alex looked up to see his guard peering through the grate.

"Captain Bernard's here to question you, Yankee."

Captain Bernard? Annabelle's fiancé. He'd have to be careful what he said.

The guard unlocked the door. Bernard removed his plumed hat before entering the confined space and covered his nose and mouth with a handkerchief.

"I'll be right outside, sir," the guard said.

Bernard motioned for Alex to remain seated, then dusted off the opposite bench before settling on it. He watched Alex for a moment before lowering the handkerchief.

After sniffing disdainfully, he said, "I know who you are Captain Alexander Hart."

Alex tensed. *Had* Annabelle told him, or did this man know his father?

When he didn't speak, Bernard went on, "I know you were once engaged to my Annabelle."

"I'm afraid you're mistaken, sir," Alex lied. "I've never been engaged and don't know anyone named Annabelle."

Bernard frowned. "You're in a heap of trouble

already, sir. One of our fine soldiers has evidence against you and will be bringing it to the colonel's attention first thing tomorrow. Furthermore, I won't sully my fiancée's sensibilities by bringing her here to identify you. And, I don't need to. I saw her talking to you when she was here. She kissed your cheek." Bernard's gaze narrowed. "Were you making plans with her? I don't take lightly to those who bother my property. When I see her again, I *will* find out if she still has feelings for you. I will *not* be betrayed again."

His mocking smile showed his true feelings. "However, if you *were* engaged to my lovely Annabelle, it seems the best man won." He rose and left. The guard locked the door after him.

If the man had meant to rile him, it hadn't worked. Katie was the only woman Alex cared about now.

And she was also the soldier who'd produced the evidence against him.

****

Katie cried for hours until she had no more tears left. Patrick tried to comfort her, but she sent him away.

He would only gloat over the fact the man she'd cared for—the man she'd hoped would replace the empty space in her heart left by Rory—was the enemy.

Alex had been kind and protective. And, given the circumstances, he'd lied by necessity.

Holy Mother of God. Was she trying to convince herself to have pity for the man? The Yankees were no better than the British soldiers back in Ireland. The men who'd laughed at her the day she'd nearly drowned. If it hadn't been for her brother pulling her out of the river...

Alex Hart deserved whatever he got...but his hands had been so tender and loving, his eyes filled with desire when he'd molded his body to hers.

How would she live with herself if he was sent to prison or executed? His death wouldn't bring back Rory or the babe.

"Lass, are you all right?"

She looked outside. Patrick stood by her tent.

"Captain Bernard questioned the prisoner. The private guarding him told me Hart's a Virginia gentleman, the son of a plantation owner."

The revelation confused Katie. "Then why would he aide the Yankees?"

"Fer sure he has his reasons."

"Aye." Katie had the sudden urge to talk to Alex. Find out what those reasons were.

"Do you have the evidence fer the captain?" Patrick asked.

"Aye, 'tis in me pack."

"See to it that the captain gets it first thing tomorrow." Patrick eyed her. "Are you sure yer all right?"

Katie knew her face was tear-streaked and swollen. But learning the man she'd come to love was a Yankee and possibly a spy would surely account for that. "I need me privacy right now."

He hesitated. "If there's anything I can do fer you, lass..."

She shook her head. "No. I'll see you in the morning."

After he left, she made her decision.

She dug the dispatch from her pack. Emerging from her tent, she moved to the fire pit and stood gazing at the flames. She held the paper out and let it fall burning to cinders. Now, there was no evidence against Alex.

But Patrick knew.

She had to free Alex and get him out of camp *tonight*.

****

Alex fell into a restless sleep, awaking in the midst of a dream. He held Katie in his arms, her curls tousled, her gray eyes bright.

"I'll stand watch fer you," she said.

He opened his eyes, realizing he was still in the guardhouse. The voice had come from outside.

"Much appreciate it, Sean," a man's voice said. "I promise I won't take long."

"Take yer time," Katie said.

Alex rose and peered through the door's grate. Katie stood outside watching the soldier who'd stood guard amble away.

She turned toward Alex, holding a finger to her lips. "I'll explain everything later. Right now, I've got to get you out of here."

Alex watched as she produced a key. She took a quick glance over her shoulder, then unlocked the door.

"I know a way to get by the pickets."

Alex had a million questions but now wasn't the time. They had to run, and fast, before the guard, or anyone else, saw them.

Taking his hand, she led him into the woods. She guided him, under cover of darkness, to a spot where they could circle around and evade the pickets.

With no moon to light the way, Alex had trouble seeing his hand in front of his face. The strong scent of pine and fetid soil told him they'd gone deep into the woods.

"Where are you taking me?" he asked.

"There are some caves on the other side of the hill we can make by dawn on foot. We can hide in one during the day."

"Caves?" Alex stiffened. He couldn't go into a cave. Just the idea sent sweat breaking the surface of his skin. "Isn't there somewhere else we could go?"

"After searching the camp fer you, the soldiers

will check the woods and the nearby town. By the time they get as far as the caves, it'll be nightfall, and we'll be on our way."

What she said made sense, but primal fear made Alex resist. Entering a cave had to be far worse than anything the Rebels could to do him. As unreasonable as it was, he couldn't shake the terror of being lost in a cave as a boy. He'd go as far as the cave with her, but then they'd have to part company. He could never set foot in a cave again.

****

Katie led Alex through the woods. She knew this area like the back of her hand and had no trouble navigating in the darkness. Her duties delivering and retrieving mail had given her the freedom to explore the Northwestern Virginia countryside. They'd spend the day resting in the caves, then head north. She hadn't yet decided where they'd go. She just knew she had to save him as he'd saved her.

They maneuvered through the forest. A flash of light followed by a thunderclap set her teeth on edge. Hopefully, they could make it to the caves before the storm broke.

"Let's hurry," she urged Alex. "We've still a long way to go."

Lightning lit the sky, and the rumble of thunder grew louder. In her mind, she imagined the guard coming back and finding them gone.

What would Patrick think?

A blinding fork of lightning followed by a deafening clap of thunder caused the ground to sizzle around them. The blast struck a large tree and sent it crashing to the ground, not far from where they stood.

"We have to get out of here," Alex said.

"Aye," Katie agreed. "This way."

They raced through the woods. Rain, falling from the sky in buckets, soaked them to the skin.

Moving as quickly as possible over the slick forest bed, they arrived at the foot of a large, rocky hill.

"There!" Katie pointed to the base of the hill where Alex could just make out a series of dark openings.

Alex halted and stared at the cave entrance.

Katie moved around him to the mouth of the nearest cave. She poked her head inside and tried to gauge the length and width, but needed a match. To escape the driving rain, she ducked in, unheedful of any creature that occupied this domain.

She struck a match against the heel of her brogan, then stretched her arm in front of her. The mouth opened into a large room. She didn't see any bear or other animals. This would be perfect.

She turned, only then realizing Alex hadn't followed.

****

Alex stood rooted to the ground. Rain plastered his hair and clothing to his body. When Katie had disappeared inside that hole, he found it impossible to draw a breath.

He'd faced bullets from both armies and discovery by the Rebels, but he couldn't face this. His breathing grew ragged and he thought he might pass out.

Katie's face appeared at the mouth of the cave. She frowned.

"Alex, come inside." She motioned to him.

He shook his head. "I can't."

A huge bolt of lightning exploded several feet from him. He nearly jumped out of his skin.

"You've got to come in," Katie urged.

Forcing one leg in front of the other, he moved toward her. She emerged and dragged him to the hole.

"No," Alex said, "I can't."

"You can and you will," Katie ordered. She

pushed him in ahead of her.

When he straightened, he bumped his head on the rock above him and swore. Katie guided him to where he could stand upright. The yawning blackness before him threatened to send him bolting back out into the storm.

Katie moved ahead of him and lit a match. "See, there're no animals in here. We can hide until nightfall."

His mouth too dry to respond, he felt sure she heard the frantic beating of his heart.

"'Tis all right," she said. "I've candles and lint in me pack. I saw a small pile of wood under an outcropping. It'll be wet, but with me candles and lint, I should be able to get a fire going at the entrance."

Producing a blanket from her pack, she handed it to him. "Dry yerself. I'll be right back with the wood."

Katie disappeared, leaving him alone in the dark. He clutched her blanket around him, shaking as his mind drifted back to the day he'd been ten years old and had tried to save Samuel.

****

Katie crouched in the outcropping and gathered enough wood to build a small fire. True, it was wet, but not all the way through. She'd cut away the damp bark with her knife.

Returning to the cave, she found Alex still stood where she'd left him. She dropped the wood by the entrance. After striking a match, she searched her pack for candles, planted one in the dirt, then lit it.

She studied Alex and frowned. His eyes looked glazed, and he was shaking.

"I'll be getting the fire started," she said.

He didn't move.

She inspected the wood by candlelight, selecting the driest pieces. Using her knife, she scraped off any wet bark, then piled the wood in the cave opening, hoping any smoke would be washed away by the rain. After applying lint, she used her candle, dripping wax onto the lint-covered wood to start a small flame. She breathed on it until it caught, then sat back on her heels, admiring her work.

"See," she said, "'tis all right. Spread the blanket here by the fire, then get out of those wet clothes."

He shook his head, his eyes wide. "I can't stay here." Turning around, he dropped the blanket and tried to move around the small flame.

Katie jumped to her feet and grabbed him by his belt. "You can't go back out there!"

When he tried to pull away, she tightened her grip, desperate to keep him inside. He stilled and turned toward her.

"Ye've a fear of caves?"

His lashes lowered.

"'Tis all right. I fear the water. You saved me from that. I'll help you now."

She released him, turned, and spread the blanket by the fire. "Come, sit here. 'Tis warm, and the smoke will be drawn outside." She smiled encouragingly as she slipped off her sack coat and laid it on a rock to dry.

Alex moved slowly toward her. She unbuckled his belt, then his coat, sliding it from his shoulders.

"Come," she urged, "let's get our wet things off." She took his hand and guided him to the blanket. The feel of his large, strong hand in hers sent a pleasurable tingle down her spine. Her heartbeat quickened.

She led him to the blanket and motioned for him to sit by her side. She removed her brogans and stockings, then helped him with his.

The glazed look in his eyes was gone. He watched her intently. Liking the feel of his eyes on her, she slid her braces down and loosened her pants, easing them over her hips and kicking them off.

Wearing only her shirt and drawers, she spread her pants, both pairs of stockings and brogans to dry by the fire.

"Now, fer yer trousers," she said.

Alex reached for his braces, sliding them down his arms, then rose and loosened his pants.

Katie bit her lip. Her fingers ached to assist him. She reached for his waistband and slid the trousers over his hips and legs, leaving him clothed in his drawers and shirt as she was.

After laying out his trousers alongside hers, she turned to him, wishing she was clad in a feminine lace-trimmed chemise. "Sit by me, Alex."

He moved slowly toward her. She took his hand and guided him to the blanket. The warmth of the fire enveloped them. Her fingers explored the planes of his cheekbones and the softness of his beard. She moved closer, brushing her lips against his mouth.

His breath hitched, and he reached for her, rubbing his thumbs along her jaw line and cheeks. Angling his mouth toward her lips, his hand moved to her nape.

His lips touched hers, sending sparks through her body, then he pulled back.

"Why did you free me?" A troubled frown creased his handsome face.

"What?"

"I lied to you. I don't deserve your help."

"Shh." Running her fingers over the lines on his forehead, she tried to soothe him. "I could no more leave you to yer fate, than you could've left me. You only did what you thought was right."

His lips touched hers again, and she boldly deepened the kiss, wanting to taste him thoroughly. She reached under the tail of his shirt, running her hands over the moist skin of his chest. Together, they pulled the garment up and over his head, exposing the sprinkle of chestnut hair and fine muscles to her hungry eyes.

"Ye're a fine figure of a man, Mr. Hart."

Katie's statement brought a smile to his face. "And what have you to show me, Katie Rose?"

Heat rose in her cheeks. Even though he'd already seen her naked, this was the first time she wanted to show him all of her. Kneeling, she lifted the hem of her shirt. His smoldering gaze told her he liked what he saw.

He helped her toss the shirt aside. Tentatively, he reached out, molding his hand to her breast. "Fits my hand perfectly."

Having his hand on her in that way sent heat to her core. Moisture pooled between her legs. He angled toward her, suckling her nipple, and she arched toward him.

"Alex," she said, "I want to see all of you."

His eyes ablaze, he stood, sliding out of his drawers.

"Ye're magnificent." She couldn't help but stare at the hard planes of his body and his throbbing need.

Taking her hands, he helped her to her feet. Releasing the tapes, he slid her drawers down until they pooled around her.

His heated gaze roamed over her, and the urge to touch him overwhelmed her. She reached for him, stroking his smooth hardness while her insides coiled, ready to explode.

****

Alex couldn't tear his gaze from Katie. The sight of her slender body and rosy skin made it impossible for him to contain himself. He'd longed to lie with her for months. Could he really be that fortunate to finally have her?

"Katie Rose, you're beautiful."

She blushed a becoming shade of pink as his gaze roved from her lovely face, down her ivory throat, to her breasts. His gaze feasted on the white mounds adorned with strawberry-colored nipples. His gaze drifted lower, down the plane of her stomach to her tiny waist, slim hips, shapely legs and triangle of fiery curls between them.

Heat seared his body. He stepped toward her and embraced her, reveling in her softness against him. A growl rose low in his throat.

She stood on her toes and took his mouth. Their lips intertwined. She tasted of the fresh apples they'd eaten earlier. Her velvety tongue licked his lips, and he guided her down to the blanket.

Needing to sample all of her, he kissed and licked his way from her swollen lips, down her satiny throat and breasts, suckling on a peaked nipple. She moaned in appreciation.

"Oh, Alex," she said. "I love you."

Shocked at her declaration—he'd thought she hated everything he stood for—he realized he loved this feisty Irishwoman, too.

"I love you, Katie Rose and want you now, if you'll have me."

"Aye." She smiled up at him, pure pleasure written on her face. "I want you, too."

Emboldened, now that she'd at long last given him permission, he stroked the sensitive spot between her legs, drawing excited gasps from her.

"Now, Alex," she said. "I need you now."

****

Katie lay panting beneath Alex's hard form. *Have mercy!* She'd never felt this with Rory, and she'd never lain with another.

His hard need stroked her belly, then moved down to enter her sensitized folds, wringing a gasp from her. She reached up to enfold him in her arms. His rhythm drove into her, bringing her waves of pleasure. She lifted her hips and legs, molding her throbbing body to his.

He shuddered, gasping, his hot breath against her face. Her body arched, and she shattered into a million pieces.

Afterward, she held him never wanting to let him go.

Chapter Thirteen

Katie awoke, enclosed in Alex's arms. Only glowing embers remained from the fire she'd built. Her blanket wrapped around them both. He must have pulled the covering over their bodies to ward off the chill.

Best get up and see what time of day it is. Preparing to rise and get dressed, she pushed his arm from where it nestled across her waist.

His body trembled. Glancing down at him, she noted his eyes were closed. Was he dreaming?

"Samuel," he rasped.

"Alex." She nudged him.

"Samuel, we've got to get out, or we'll die."

Katie shook him again. "Wake up."

His eyes popped open. He jerked, then relaxed and sighed.

"You were having a nightmare." Katie tucked the blanket around them. "You called someone named Samuel."

His eyes widened. "I was dreaming about..."

"What?" She waited, wanting to know what frightened him so.

"It was a long time ago," he said thickly.

She ran her hand over his moist chest then down his arm, grasping his hand.

"Please, tell me."

He watched her a moment as if trying to decide whether to honor her request. "I was ten. Samuel was one of my father's slaves."

"Yer father kept slaves?" Revulsion coursed through her. She tensed waiting for the rest of the story.

"My father owned a plantation near Richmond. Samuel was thirteen. I grew up with him. Thought of him as a friend." He stopped. She snuggled against him and kissed his cheek.

"What happened to him?"

"My older sister accused him of sneaking into her room and stealing her earrings. I knew he didn't do it and told her so."

Her gaze drifted over him. She tried to imagine him as a young boy. "Yer sister didn't believe you?"

He shook his head. "My father didn't either. He took Samuel to the barn and whipped him, leaving gashes in his skin."

Katie winced.

"So, I took him away from there."

"Where did you go?"

"I knew of some caves near our plantation. I thought he could hide there, and I'd bring him food."

His heart thudded against her breasts. "What happened?"

"The cave we hid in had a number of rooms. Samuel wanted to go all the way in so he'd feel safe. When I tried to leave, I couldn't find the way out."

She caught her breath, waiting for him to continue.

"We were lost for two days." He shook his head. "I was sure we were going to die. On the second day, Samuel's father found us."

"Aye." She nodded, understanding now. "That's why you fear caves." When he didn't respond, she asked, "And what happened to Samuel after that?"

"My father sold him, and I never saw him again."

Katie sighed. "Is that why you spy fer the Yankees?"

"One of the reasons."

She pressed her ear to his chest, listening to the

comforting sound of his heartbeat. "I'm sorry I turned you in."

"But you had to—"

She placed her fingers against his lips to halt his protest. How could she have doubted him after he'd saved her life? He kissed each of her fingers, and the softness of his lips made them tingle. Wrapping her arms around his hard body, she kissed his lips, and he held her, taking possession of her mouth. His throbbing need pressed against her stomach, and they made love again.

****

Alex sighed and held Katie against his chest. He longed to stay this way forever, but they had to get moving.

"Katie, darlin'." He nudged her shoulder. "We have to get up."

She startled awake, eyeing him. "Aye. What time is it?"

He glanced toward the cave mouth. "Looks like the sun is going down."

Alex rose and offered his hand to help her to her feet. He retrieved the blanket and draped it over her shoulders. Retrieving his clothes from one of the rocks, he climbed into them. By the time he tied up his brogans, she had fastened her braces and retrieved her shoes and stockings.

"Alex." She pulled on one of her brogans. "I've been thinking about where we should go."

He glanced at her in surprise. "What are you planning?"

"Go north, I'm thinking. Into Maryland, then Pennsylvania."

Alex hesitated. "I need to go to Washington."

She lowered her lashes. "We could escape the war. Start over."

He watched her tie her shoes. "I can't do that, darlin'. I have an obligation to report. And I'm long overdue."

She stood and turned away from him. Lifting her sack coat, she shook the garment out.

"I can't abandon my mission," he said to her back.

She stiffened, then shrugged into her coat. When she turned to face him, her eyes narrowed.

"I'm sorry, Katie."

"I saved you just so you could go back to the Yankee army?"

He stepped toward her, and she backed away. He reached out to her. "You can come with me to Washington."

She shook her head, sending her curls bouncing as she buttoned her coat. "I can't. I've a duty, too."

"To the Confederates?" He couldn't believe what she was saying.

"I took an oath."

"But—"

"I'm goin' back to the 2nd Virginia." Avoiding his eyes, she folded her blanket, stuffing it into her pack.

"You can't do that. They'll know you helped me escape."

She smiled, but he could read the tension in her face. "I'll say you tricked me—lied to me. Then you forced me to go with you." She met his gaze. "Then I hit you over the head and got away."

He sighed. "What if they don't believe you?"

"They will."

He eyed her doubting they would.

"Patrick will believe me and back up me story."

His heart sank at the thought of losing her. He couldn't allow her to do this.

"Please, come with me to Washington. There's nothing for you back in camp."

Her face hardened. "I swore an oath to avenge me family. I know why you feel the way you do, but I can't turn on me own family."

In the end, she refused to budge. He had no choice but to leave her.

****

Maurice paced before his tent on the warm, clear night. Sergeant O'Reilly stood at attention.

"I want to know," Maurice said through gritted teeth, "where your traitor brother went with that Yankee spy."

"I'm sorry, sir," Patrick replied. "I wouldn't be knowing that."

"I don't believe you, Sergeant," Maurice spat. "I think you know where they are."

"Begging yer pardon, *sir*, but I was on picket when the Yankee escaped. When I returned, me brother was nowhere to be found."

Maurice took a deep breath. He glared at the sergeant.

O'Reilly didn't flinch when Maurice moved within an inch of his face.

"I need to know..." Maurice lowered his voice, his tone menacing. "...of any word from your brother. Do you hear me, Sergeant?"

"Yes, sir."

"Dismissed."

After the sergeant left, Maurice seethed. He'd lost his prize because of that Irish boy and by God, the lad was going to pay.

****

Katie woke on her blanket alone. After Alex left, she'd decided to spend the night in the cave and return to camp in the morning.

When he'd asked her to go to Washington, she'd been sorely tempted, but memories of Rory kept her from abandoning her post. Had she done the right thing? Nothing could bring Rory or the babe back.

And Alex loved her.

Slowly, she tied on her brogans and rolled her

blanket, stuffing it into her pack. Only one thing left to do now; go back to camp and hope Patrick believed her lies.

She hefted her pack for the hike back but nearly sank back to the floor of the cave, her stomach in knots. She'd lost everything that mattered again, and this time it was her own fault.

When Katie approached the camp pickets, she knew she was in a lot of trouble. Grady's eyes widened, and he glanced at the other soldier standing guard.

"I didn't reckon to see you back anytime soon," Grady said. "I have orders to escort you to the captain."

Katie tensed. "Captain Bernard?" The last thing she wanted was to face the steely-eyed officer. The man didn't sit well with her.

"No," she protested. "Ye've got to allow me to see Patrick first."

"Sorry, Sean," Grady said. "Orders is orders."

"Please, Grady," she pleaded. "You know me. I've got to speak to me brother first."

Grady exchanged glances with the other picket. "Reckon I can send for him before I take you in."

"Thank you, Grady." Although she'd won this battle, she didn't know if she'd be able to convince Patrick of her innocence.

And she still had to face the captain.

****

Grady allowed Patrick to guard her so the two could converse in private.

Katie waited as Patrick paced the hard-packed earth. His hardened expression told her he needed time to get out what he wanted to say.

"Why did you do it? Did he promise you his undying love if you helped him?" He stroked his beard, eyeing her intently. "Did he soil you?"

She squirmed under his gaze. "Patrick! How can

you ask me that?"

"He's a Yankee. Everything we've learned to despise." His eyelids narrowed to slits. "You haven't forgotten what they did to Rory, me father, yer babe?"

"Hush, Patrick." Katie glanced around. "Someone might hear you."

"Ye've aided the enemy." He clasped his hands behind his back and continued to pace. "That makes you a traitor and casts suspicion on me."

"He tricked me," she said. "He said he was innocent, that the dispatch wasn't his."

"His name was on it," Patrick pointed out.

Heat rose to her cheeks. She'd forgotten about that.

"Where is the dispatch now?"

Katie chewed on her lower lip. "I burned it."

"Burned it, you say?"

"So, you see," she rushed on, "there's no evidence."

Patrick grasped her arm. "You helped a prisoner escape, burned evidence, and deserted yer post."

"He forced me. He'd of killed me if I hadn't escaped."

"Katie, love." He shook his head. "I fear I don't believe you. You were seduced by a spy, and now ye've got to face the consequences."

Her heart hammered in her chest. "What are you goin' to do?"

He raised his arm in a signal to Grady. "Ye've left me no choice but to turn you in."

****

Maurice paced before the boy, who sat on a camp stool flanked on each side by guards. The lad was smaller than he'd realized. He sat rigidly, hands on his lap, eyes downcast. His brother, who'd brought him in, stood at attention.

"At ease, Sergeant," Maurice said.

Sergeant O'Reilly relaxed but kept his gaze directed at his brother.

"Private O'Reilly," Maurice said. "I order you to tell me where you left Alexander Hart."

"In a cave on the other side of the forest, sir," the lad said.

Maurice leaned in close. "Is he still there?"

"No, sir. He left yesterday."

"Yesterday?" His blood heated. *That son-of-a-bitch. I'll never catch him now.*

"Where was he going?" Maurice asked.

"I wouldn't be knowing that, sir."

Maurice stroked his chin, considering his options. He'd lost his prize, but he could still take out his revenge on the boy. He nodded. "We may not catch *him*, but we have you."

The lad's eyes grew huge as their gazes met.

Maurice smiled.

"Sir," the sergeant protested, "he's but a lad."

"He's aided the enemy, Sergeant. We need to make an example of him."

The lad's mouth gaped as he turned pleading eyes on the sergeant. He frowned, but saluted and left.

Bernard studied the boy, contemplating how he'd enjoy making him suffer.

****

Federal Headquarters
Washington, D.C.

Alex sat in the office of Colonel Tinneman and gazed out the window at Federal soldiers and civilians strolling the city sidewalks. Carriages clattered down the streets.

He brushed a bit of lint from his blue military frock coat and awaited the colonel's arrival.

"Alex."

He turned toward the corridor at the sound of a familiar voice.

"Elliot." He rose to greet his friend, Dr. Elliot James. Admiring Elliot's uniform, he said, "I see you've finally earned the rank of captain."

"So I have," Elliot said. "Means I no longer have to 'sir' you."

Alex laughed. "If you recall, in the beginning of the war, I had to 'sir' you."

"And now we're equals." Elliot's nut-brown eyes appraised him. "How goes it with you?"

"Surviving."

"That bad." Elliot glanced around. "Come see me after you've spoken to the colonel. I'll buy you lunch."

Elliot ducked out leaving Alex alone to wait and contemplate his situation. Seeing his old friend again was a pleasure. Elliot had taken him in after Annabelle had jilted him and his family had disowned him. He'd followed Elliot into the Union Army serving as a private and worked up to the rank of lieutenant before being recruited as a Federal spy. Since then, Alex had spent most of his time alone, unable to trust anyone.

Katie had opened up a part of him he'd thought dead. He'd barely slept since returning to Washington, even though the trip had exhausted him. He'd walked part of the way, then hired a local farmer to take him to the nearest train station.

Yes, he was now safely back in Washington, but he needed to know what had happened to Katie. He'd be unable to rest until he found out.

****

Katie lay on the hard bench in the guardhouse, awaiting Captain Bernard's interrogation. She had no one to blame for her predicament, since Alex had offered to take her with him to Washington. She should have gone. Now, she'd likely be sent to prison.

She couldn't blame Patrick, either. He'd done

what he did to protect himself. She couldn't expect him to take the fall for her mistake.

When the guard came for her, she took a deep breath, trying to slow her erratic pulse. The captain scared her. He seemed evil.

After he unlocked and opened the door, the guard stepped aside to allow her to emerge. She stepped out, but he stopped her with a coarse hand on her chest.

"I've orders to search you before taking you to the captain."

"Search me?" Katie felt the blood drain from her face. How thorough of a search did this man intend?

"Captain's orders."

She spread her arms. "For what would you be looking for?"

The guard sneered. "Evidence on your person...hidden weapons."

"I'll empty all me pockets right in front of you," she said. "There's no need to search me."

"I have my orders. Remove your coat."

Katie unbuttoned and removed her sack coat, handing it to him for inspection. When he tore out the seam, Katie protested. "That's me only coat!"

Dropping the garment to the ground at his feet, the guard stomped on it. "That's what I do with traitor's coats."

Katie stared open-mouthed at the man. How dare he?

"Now," he said, "remove your braces."

"What?"

"You heard me."

Holy Mother of God! What does he mean to do?

Gulping, Katie lowered her braces. Her trousers slid to her hips. When the guard reached for her, she tensed. She stuffed her hands into her pockets, turning them inside-out.

"See," she said, "no weapons."

Ignoring her statement, he reached for her hips. She flushed and licked her lips. When he reached her crotch, she gasped.

His puzzled gaze caught hers. "What are you...a eunuch?" He eyed her with disgust.

She didn't respond, not knowing what to say.

He reached for her chest. Although her breasts were bound, she refused to allow this crude man to touch her again. She grasped his forearm.

"I'm a woman," she said. "Keep yer filthy hands off me."

The astonished soldier eyed her up and down. "Whooee! Wait until the captain hears this."

Katie's heart raced. No one could help her now, but telling the truth had been the only way to stop the guard's assault.

"Come along, missy." He grasped her roughly by the arm. "The captain needs to hear this."

Katie shivered, wondering what Bernard would do to her.

Chapter Fourteen

The guard escorted Katie to Captain Bernard's tent. He conferred privately with Bernard, leaving her to wait.

She watched their faces and caught the guard's leer and Bernard's raised eyebrows.

After the guard took his leave, Katie tried not to cringe when the captain appraised her. Beneath his thick auburn mustache, the hint of a smirk played around his lips.

"Private Sean O'Reilly." He shook his head. "I've just been informed you aren't a lad at all. I want to know your *real* name."

Katie's heart thudded, as she wondered what fate he planned for her.

"You will tell me now!"

"'Tis Katie O'Reilly, sir."

"But your brother..." He brushed a finger over his mustache. "...if he *is* your brother. Is he a lover, perhaps?"

Katie flinched at his insinuation. "Patrick's me brother-in-law."

"I see." He leaned close. She felt the heat of his brandy-scented breath on her cheek. "He's been hiding your...abomination?"

Katie glanced up. "Me what, sir?"

His leer sent chills down her spine.

"Any *woman* who dresses as a man, fights and acts like one, cannot count herself among the fair ladies of the Confederacy whom I'm sworn to defend. You're no better than a whore." His voice lowered menacingly. "And that's how you should be treated."

Katie's blood heated, and she balled her fists. How dare this man compare her to a harlot?

The captain stood, glaring down at her. "Corporal," he called. "I want this atrocity locked up. I'll deal with her later."

"Yes, sir." The corporal entered the tent and prodded Katie. She obediently preceded him back to the guardhouse.

Once inside, she sank to the bench. Running her hands through her curls, she brought up an image of Alex. She'd never regret saving him. He was nothing like the Yankees who'd ransacked the farm. He truly wanted to help people and had defied his family to do so.

She'd never thought much about the African slaves, but her own experience as a child in Ireland gave her some perspective. The Irish had always been downtrodden both by the British in their homeland and then the Americans after they'd arrived in New York.

Recalling Alex's story of helping the slave boy when he, himself, had been a lad, Katie felt proud of what he'd done. At such a young age, he'd exhibited an incredible amount of courage. He was an honorable man, and if she ever had the chance to see him again, she planned to tell him so.

****

Federal Camp south of Gettysburg, Pennsylvania
June 30, 1863

Alex surveyed the bucolic farmland tapering off to rolling hills. The knowledge that the Rebel Army now occupied the land north of the town caused the peaceful setting to take on a nightmarish quality. Elliot approached bearing two tin mugs.

"Coffee?" he asked.

"Don't mind if I do." Alex accepted the cup. "Thank you."

"You don't seem quite yourself." Elliot pulled up

a stool and settled across from him.

Alex chewed on his lip. He hadn't mentioned Katie to *anyone*. But Elliot was his closest friend. He'd helped and guided Alex when everyone else had deserted him. If he could tell another soul, it would be Elliot.

"I met a woman in Virginia," Alex said.

Elliot nodded. "Ah, I see. Lady troubles."

"The problem is, I think she's in a heap of trouble because of me."

Elliot leaned forward, his dark eyes intense. "Do tell. Who is this woman who's affected you so?"

Alex sighed. "You wouldn't believe me if I told you."

His friend sat back, sipping his coffee, his expectant gaze focused on Alex.

"She's a Rebel soldier."

"My God!"

"Her name's Katie O'Reilly. She disguised herself as a man."

"But how on earth did you...?" Elliot seemed at a loss for words.

"I was out on a scouting mission, dressed as a civilian. I found her by a stream filling her canteen."

"Then what happened?"

"She fell into the stream. Couldn't swim. I jumped in and pulled her out." He couldn't suppress a smile at the memory.

"And that's when you learned she was a woman?"

Alex shook his head. "No. I thought she was a boy."

Elliot smiled. "And?"

"She walloped me."

"She what?" Elliot leaned forward.

"She thought I was trying to steal her mailbag."

"Ah, she was a mail carrier."

Alex nodded. "I didn't find out she was a woman

until..."

Elliot raised a brow. "Go on, man. Until what?"

"We disrobed."

His friend stared at him, mouth agape.

"It's not what you think. We were soaking wet, and it was cold. We'd of frozen to death if we hadn't changed clothes."

Elliot waited, saying nothing.

"I've never been with a woman like Katie."

"Seems you've gotten over Miss Carswell."

"Reckon so."

"But what's happened to this soldier-woman who's entranced you so?"

"After she helped me escape, she went back to the 2nd Virginia. I wanted her to come with me, but she refused."

Elliot shook his head.

"I fear the Rebels will know she helped me and arrest her as a traitor."

"But if they find out she's a woman—"

"I don't believe that will help her." He caught his friend's concerned gaze. "It may only make things worse."

"I'm sorry, Alex. I wish there was some way I could be of help."

"I'm thankful you listened. I can't tell this story to anyone else."

"So," Elliot said, changing the subject, "how can I help with your new assignment?"

Alex stroked his beard. "You can get me a straight-edge and some shaving cream."

****

Confederate camp, north of Gettysburg
Same Day

When the Confederate Army moved north, Katie was brought along in chains. Captain Bernard wasn't ready to send her away until he'd had his fill of tormenting her. She suspected he still thought she might lead him to Alex. Once they'd arrived, the men set up a new guardhouse in camp. Katie was then locked up to await the captain's further questioning. Curling up on the narrow bench that served as her bed, she dozed.

Later, she woke and glanced at the grate in the cell door. The sky had darkened to twilight. How long had she slept? Her stomach rumbled.

"Guard," she called. "Have you got any food fer me?"

A face appeared at the grate.

The guard had changed. This man was one of her friends. "Nate?"

The young man nodded, his brown eyes puzzled. "Sean? Er...I mean, ma'am?"

Katie rose, leaning toward the grate. "I'm the same person you know as Sean."

"But...this is downright perplexing...ma'am."

"Could you please get me a bite to eat, Nate. Then we'll talk about it."

He nodded. "Yes, ma'am. Right away."

The lad hurried off. A plan began to take hold in Katie's mind.

After finishing her meal of grits and a mug of tea, Katie approached the grate. "Nate," she whispered. "I want to talk."

He moved to the grate, eyeing her. "About why you're dressed like that?"

Katie smiled. Backing up, she lifted her leg onto the bench, then reached for the hem of her trousers and pulled it up exposing her calf and ankle.

"Nate, I've always thought you to be such a handsome and strapping man."

Nate licked his lips. "You did?"

"Aye." She loosened the buttons of her shirt, arranging the fabric so he could see down to the vee of her bosom.

"Of course, I could never tell you so."

"Ma'am?" He looked ready to bolt.

She had to convince him to unlock the door. "For months, I've longed to run me hands over yer fine chest."

Nate shook his head, clearly at a loss for words.

"Open the door," she coaxed, "and I'll show you."

His brown eyes flicked back and forth. "I can't do that, ma'am."

"No one will know." She pulled at her shirt, exposing more skin. "'Tis so hot in here."

He ran a finger over his lips clearly trying to decide what to do.

Katie gave him her most encouraging smile. She hated to do this to the lad, but she had to get out of here. Bernard had something evil planned for her; she could feel it.

The keys scraped in the lock. When the door opened, he stepped inside. Katie took him into her arms. She noted his rifle propped against an oak just outside the shack. She just needed to get around him.

She brushed her lips over his cheek. He was young, but eager. "I'll show you what I've wanted to do all these long months." She pulled the hem of his shirt from his trousers, reached beneath and stroked his chest. He was a bit pudgy, but she easily faked her desire.

"Kiss me, Nate," she murmured.

His eyes widened. She took his face into her hands and kissed him thoroughly, all the time regretting taking advantage of him.

She broke off the kiss and made to move around him, but the sight of a clean-shaven man dressed in black wearing a white Roman collar, startled her. He stood watching them.

****

Alex could do nothing but stare at the man kissing *his* Katie. Her shirt was unbuttoned, exposing a great expanse of white flesh. In that moment, forgetting his assignment, he yanked the man off her and socked him in the jaw.

The soldier recovered and lurched for his rifle. Alex hit him on the back of the neck, and he slumped to the ground.

"Father?" Katie didn't recognize him.

"It's me," he rasped.

Her eyes widened. "Alex?" After a moment of studying him, she threw her arms around him.

The soft feel of her again was pure heaven. He found himself at a loss for words.

"I thought to never see you again." She glanced down. "But what have you done to poor Nate?"

"Nate?" Alex stared at her. "I thought he was attacking you."

"No, I..."

"What? Are you telling me *you* were kissing *him*?" His blood heated at the thought of her moving on to another man.

"I was tryin' to escape."

"By kissing him?"

"Aye." Anger flashed in her eyes. "And it was working until you came along and hit the poor lad."

He grasped her forearm and pulled her from the guardhouse. They couldn't stay here debating. "Come on, we've got to get out of camp. I fear I've compromised my cover."

"But what about Nate?" she protested. "You may have killed him."

Sighing, Alex knelt and felt for a pulse. The lad's breathing was regular, his pulse steady. "Reckon he'll be out for awhile, but aside from a nasty headache and some bruising, he should be all right." He rose and glanced into the guardhouse. "They'll reckon you clobbered him when he came for your dinner plate." He caught her worried gaze. "Now, let's skedaddle."

She nodded, but eyed him again. "Why are you dressed as a priest?"

"It's a disguise. I'm ministering to the Rebel soldiers." His eyes roved to the white vee of her bosom. "Button your shirt before we go. We don't want to attract any more attention."

Alex pulled his hat brim low and patted Katie on the back as if he were giving counsel. They weaved their way through rows of tents. Glancing around to be sure no one took notice of them, he led her to a spot where he thought they could slip around the pickets unnoticed.

Katie shook her head. "No, I don't think we should go this way."

"Why?" Alex wondered why she was so skittish. "I didn't see any pick—"

"Halt, or I'll shoot!" a deep voice called out.

Alex turned, exchanging glances with Katie. Her eyes were wide and her breath caught.

Before he'd spied her kissing that soldier, he'd moved freely through camp, compliments of his forged pass. Now, he was in the company of an escaped prisoner.

Chapter Fifteen

Katie stared at Alex. Her heart thumped rapidly, and she had a hard time catching her breath. She was in great trouble for sure, but what would happen to him?

Two pickets approached, rifles raised. She swallowed, trying to order her thoughts.

The soldiers, an older, black-haired man with a heavy beard, and a young, blond soldier with a bit of fuzz on his chin and upper lip, eyed Alex. Katie tensed, uncertain what to say.

Amazingly, Alex smiled.

"Gentlemen," he said, "me name is Father Flannery. I've been sent from Richmond to minister to all you fine soldiers. How can I help you men?"

Katie grimaced at the sound of his fake brogue, but the pickets didn't seem suspicious.

"You've got a pass, Padre?" the older picket asked.

"Of course, me fine man." Alex reached into his pocket and produced a paper.

The soldier squinted, studying the script.

"You'll find everything in order, sir," Alex said.

The soldier stared at Katie. "And who's this you've got with you?"

Alex winked at her and smiled, easing her fear. Maybe he could pull this off, after all.

"'Tis a young man I'm ministering to. His sainted mother asked me to look in on him."

"You look familiar." The soldier moved close to Katie. His pungent breath caused her nose to crinkle. "What's your name, son?"

"Sean Coyne," she said quickly, giving her maiden surname.

The man scratched his beard. "Don't recall hearin' that name." He glanced at his younger partner. "How 'bout you, Jimmy. You hear tell of Sean here."

While the younger man appraised her, Katie fought desperately to control her breathing.

His eyes widened. "I know who you are." He raised his rifle. "You're the woman soldier turned traitor."

Katie's heart plummeted to her stomach.

****

Alex's mind raced. He had to see them out of this. "Gentlemen," he said, "I can assure you yer mistaken about this lad." He patted Katie's shoulder. She trembled beneath his hand. He squeezed gently to steady her.

Jimmy kept his rifle aimed at them, while the older soldier whispered something in his ear.

"You'll have to stay here with Jimmy," he said, "while I find an officer to straighten this out."

"There's no need fer that, sir," Alex protested.

"I apologize, Padre. We'll get this fixed up right quick." He started to move off, but another soldier appeared and halted him.

Alex flinched as he recognized Patrick O'Reilly. The situation was going from bad to worse.

"What's the problem here, Corporal?" O'Reilly asked.

The corporal pointed at Alex and Katie. "She may be an escaped prisoner, Sergeant. And the Padre was aiding her. I've got to fetch an officer."

"I'll be only to glad to escort them to the captain," O'Reilly said.

Alex glanced at Katie, who warily watched her brother-in-law. What had happened between them since she'd returned?

The pickets seemed relieved to be rid of them and returned to their posts.

O'Reilly motioned for them to precede him. Alex needed to come up with a plan to get Katie out of this camp. Could he overpower O'Reilly without more soldiers interfering? He didn't think so.

Once they were out of sight of the pickets, O'Reilly ordered them to halt. He moved close to Katie and gently stroked her cheek.

"Katie, lass, forgive me. I never should have turned you in."

Katie's gaze met his. Alex watched, unsure what was happening.

"Patrick, I—"

"Shh," he soothed. "Ah, lass, I was angry. And jealous." He glanced at Alex. "Yes, I know who you are...though I didn't recognize you earlier."

Alex tensed, swearing under his breath.

O'Reilly turned back to Katie. "I love you, lass, and I don't want to see you come to any harm. I want you to be happy, even if it has to be with this Yankee."

"Patrick, what are you saying?" Katie stared at him.

A rustling sound in the brush signaled someone approaching. O'Reilly motioned for Alex and Katie to crouch in the brush. He re-directed the soldier who'd come to relieve himself.

Once the man left, O'Reilly ordered, "Stay here. Don't let anyone see you. I'll be back."

After he'd gone, Alex whispered to Katie, "Why is he helping us?"

She shook her head. "I don't know. Patrick was the one who turned me in."

"He what?" Anger heated his blood. How could her own relative have betrayed her?

"I can't be blaming him. He felt about the Yankees as I do...did." Her gaze locked on his.

136

"Helping you escape and running off with you..."

Alex nodded. "He's jealous. Did you know?"

"That he was in love with me?" Katie shook her head. "I had no idea. He's always treated me like his sister."

"Apparently that's changed." Alex didn't blame the man. If he had the beautiful Irish Rebel at his side day after day, he would never have been able to resist her for so long. Of course, she *was* O'Reilly's brother's widow.

"Are you sure he's going to help us?" he asked.

She nodded. "I believe he will." She smiled, causing his breath to catch. "And he gave us his blessings."

"In a roundabout way, I suppose he did."

Hearing footsteps approach, Alex gathered Katie close. He buried his face in her hair and inhaled her scent. He never wanted to leave her again.

Patrick crouched to confer with them. Alex still wasn't sure he trusted the man, but he really didn't have any other choice.

"I've got Morna and a mare for Alex you can use to escape and a few supplies waiting just outside camp. Follow me, and I'll get you to them."

"Patrick, I—"

He cut Katie off. "No need to speak now, lass. I've got to get you out before the camp is searched."

He led them through the wooded area, skirting around the tents to avoid being spotted. When they reached the mares, O'Reilly turned to Katie.

"Patrick," she said, "how can I ever—"

He pressed his lips against hers for a chaste kiss. "Be happy, lass, and may the wind be always at yer back."

He turned to Alex and extended a hand. Alex shook his hand firmly.

"Take care of the lass, and Godspeed." Patrick backed away, turned, walked a few yards then

stopped dead.

Katie's gasp drew Alex's gaze to the tall man standing beside Patrick. *Maurice Bernard. How in blazes can we have such bad luck?*

Alex drew Katie into the brush behind the rail where the horses were tethered and motioned her to silence.

"Just what is going on here, Sergeant?" Bernard demanded. "That woman prisoner you brought me has escaped, and now I hear tell a priest helped her?"

"I wouldn't be knowing anything about that, sir."

"I'm afraid I don't believe you, Sergeant." Bernard took a last puff on his cigar and moved toward Alex and Katie's hiding spot.

Alex sucked in his breath. Bernard gazed around as if searching for something, then carelessly tossed his cigar butt at Katie's feet. She fell back, shaking the underbrush and drawing Bernard's glare.

"Who's there?" Bernard's boot nearly connected with Katie's chin.

Alex rose, shielding her from the captain.

"What do we have here?" Bernard glowered at Patrick. "I do hope you weren't aiding an escaped prisoner, Sergeant?"

"I was the one aiding her," Alex said.

"You?" Bernard's eyes widened with recognition. "Well, it seems we have two escaped prisoners. Good work, Sergeant."

"Yes, sir." Patrick bowed his head.

****

Katie could scarcely draw a breath. This was all going wrong.

Bernard pulled his revolver and motioned for her and Alex to precede him. "I'll take these prisoners back myself, Sergeant. You may return to your post."

Patrick stood motionless. Katie tried to fathom what he was thinking. He'd almost gotten them away.

Bernard herded them past Patrick.

Katie caught his gaze. Despair and regret furrowed his brow. Once she was past him, his cry caused her to twist around.

"No!" Patrick's hoarse voice caused all three to turn. "Ye'll not be taking them anywhere, sir."

Patrick's rifle leveled at Bernard.

"I see." Bernard glanced at each of them. "You're all in this together." He leveled his pistol at Patrick. "I'll see all of you hang."

Everything seemed to happen in slow motion.

Bernard aimed his revolver at Patrick. Alex lunged at Bernard's back and a gunshot rang out. Patrick fell.

Katie rushed to her brother-in-law's side. Blood oozed from his shoulder. "Oh, Patrick!" she cried.

She turned to find Bernard holding his gun on Alex. Alex raised his arms in surrender.

"This is fer you, lass," Patrick whispered. He raised his rifle and another blast caused her to jump. Bernard collapsed, crumpling forward onto his face.

"Get away, Katie," Patrick rasped, "before the others come to see what the shots were about."

"But, Patrick..." She couldn't leave him like this. Her chest tightened, and she wanted to sob.

"Get on those horses and run. Run as fast as you can."

Katie's vision clouded. She couldn't leave him to die.

Alex made the decision for her. He pulled her to her feet. "Come on, we haven't much time."

****

Katie patted Morna's muzzle, then mounted. She'd been shocked by Patrick's behavior. How long had he felt as he did? She'd never suspected he'd had those feelings for her.

Alex settled onto the other mare. "We'd best skedaddle before we're spotted."

Moving through the cover of trees and undergrowth, Alex led her away from camp. "Gettysburg is to the south, we should head north."

She nodded, willing to follow wherever he led.

After advancing several yards, Alex halted, motioning her to stop also. "Did you hear that?"

"What?" She glanced around, her heartbeat racing.

"I think there's someone over—" He pointed to her right. "—there."

She glanced over her shoulder, then squinted and could make out someone in a brown hat and coat. "'Tis a picket."

"Damnation!" he exclaimed. "We're going in the wrong direction." He pointed to the left. "Follow me, and don't stop no matter what happens."

Heat rose to her cheeks, and her pulse surged. She wheeled her mare around. Alex broke into a gallop, and she followed. They whipped through the woods and out into the clearing passing a handful of startled soldiers.

Katie didn't look back even when she heard, "Halt!"

A shotgun blast sounded.

Alex cried out. He slumped to the side, and she realized he'd been shot.

Knowing they couldn't stop for more than a few seconds, she pulled Morna alongside his mare and quickly mounted behind him.

"Hold on!" she cried.

Another blast rang out.

Katie hated to leave Morna behind but slapped her on the rump to send her back, hoping to keep her out of harm's way.

She reached around Alex to grasp the reins.

It wouldn't be easy to hold him upright and ride, but she had no choice.

They had only one place they could go.

Chapter Sixteen

Katie raced around the outskirts of town toward the Federal camp to the south. Alex's body went slack. She had a hard time keeping him on the horse. She feared he'd fall. Squeezing his arm to be sure he was alive, she forced a groan from him.

"Hold on." Her breath caught when she noticed the amount of blood covering her trousers. "Mother of God!" She slowed at the sight of a soldier in blue.

"Halt!" he cried.

Reining in the mare, she raised her left arm and held onto Alex with her right. "This man needs help."

Two soldiers warily approached. One held his rifle on her, while the other circled around to Alex.

"This here's a priest," he said.

The other soldier, a brown-haired man with streaks of gray and a web of wrinkles puckering his face, studied her. "You look like a Reb. Where'd ya come from?"

Katie decided truth would be the best policy to get Alex help quickly. "The Confederate camp north of town. He was rescuing me."

The soldier's eyes widened. "Rescuing you?"

"I gave aid to a Federal spy."

A groan from Alex brought Katie's patience to the limit. "He needs a doctor. Now! Please, help him."

While the second soldier, a slim, red-haired boy supported Alex, the older soldier rounded on Katie.

"Where's this Federal spy?" he asked.

Inclining her head toward Alex, Katie said, "*He's*

the spy."

"The priest?" The soldier's eyes narrowed.

"He's not a priest. He's a Federal soldier."

"Fetch the surgeon," he said to the younger man. To Katie, he said, "You—get down off that horse."

The young soldier raced away. Katie glanced down at the other man. "I'll do me best, but I don't want him to fall. Won't you hold him up, while I slide down?"

The soldier studied her a moment. He seemed unsure.

"I swear I'll stay right here. I only want to get help fer this man."

When he nodded, she turned to whisper to Alex. "It will be all right. Ye'll be seeing the doctor."

Lifting her leg, she awkwardly slid down while the soldier supported Alex. Once she was on the ground, he slumped forward resting against the mare's mane.

The soldier pointed the barrel of his rifle at her. She raised her hands. "I don't have a weapon."

He glanced from her to Alex. She feared he'd fall to the ground if help didn't come soon.

The young soldier returned accompanied by a dark-haired officer. The man turned Alex's face toward him. "Alex!"

"You know him, Doc?" the older soldier asked.

"Yes, this is Captain Hart. Take him back to my tent."

The red-haired soldier took the reins of the mare while the older man held his rifle on Katie. She watched in relief as the doctor and the young soldier led Alex away.

"You're comin' with me, Reb," the older man said.

"I'll be giving you no trouble." In truth, she didn't care what happened to her now, as long as Alex was all right.

****

July 1, 1863

Alex groaned and opened his eyes. His side felt like he had a bayonet stuck inside him. A nearby blast jolted him. He nearly slid off the narrow cot.

"What the devil's going on?" he asked.

A steward rushed by carrying a basin of red-tinged water.

The young, blond-haired man stopped and eyed Alex. "The battle's begun, sir."

"Battle?" Alex tried to recall where he'd last been. He'd gone to the Confederate camp and found Katie. "Where am I?"

"Federal camp, sir."

"*Federal* camp? How'd I get here?"

"A Reb soldier brought you in. You'd been shot in the side."

Alex reached a hand under his shirt and felt heavy bandages.

"Doc dug the bullet out and stitched you up."

"Where's the doctor?"

"I'll fetch him for you right quick, sir." The young man hurried off.

If Katie had brought him here, where was she now?

"You're awake, thank God." Elliot leaned over him and inspected the bandages wrapped around his torso.

"Reckon you're the man who put me back together."

Elliot lifted a dark brow. "I wouldn't say you're put back together just yet. But you're lucky your friend brought you here in time. You've lost a great deal of blood."

"That was Katie. Where is she?"

Elliot's mouth gaped. "You mean to say, that red-headed Rebel lad was your Irish warrior-woman?"

Alex grinned. "One and the same."

Elliot frowned. "I'm sorry."

"What?" Alex couldn't fathom why Elliot was apologizing. "Why?"

"I don't know where the pickets have taken her."

Alex grasped Elliot's sleeve. "You've got to find her. I don't want her coming to any harm."

"I'll do my very best, my friend."

After Elliot left, Alex lay back worrying what had become of her. If he weren't so weak, he'd get up off this damned cot and search for her himself.

****

The guards escorted Katie through the Federal camp and deposited her into an open pen where a group of Confederate soldiers captured in battle awaited their fate.

"In you go, Reb." The guard prodded her, shoving her in among the other prisoners. Although she hadn't cared what happened to her earlier, she worried about Alex. She had no way of knowing if he still lived.

A chestnut-haired boy with a face full of freckles, caught her eye. He looked too young to be in the army. He watched her warily.

"Did they catch you in the battle, too?" he asked, moving closer.

"No...I had to get help fer another soldier who'd been shot."

The lad nodded eagerly. "So did my pa. They done took him to the Yankee hospital. I don't rightly know if he'll be all right, though."

Katie could read the fear in the young man's light blue eyes. "What's yer name, lad, and how old are you?"

"My name's Caleb, and I'll be twelve next week."

Katie repressed a shudder. He was just a babe. "Why are you here? You weren't in the ranks."

"I'm a drummer," he explained. "But the

Yankees took my drum."

Sympathizing with his loss, Katie said, "You can get another one."

He shook his head. "I don't know. Maybe when Pa comes back..." His face crumpled.

She rested an arm on his shoulder. "Your da will be all right." Even as she said it, she feared she was lying to the lad. How could she guarantee anything? She didn't know if Alex would survive.

Glancing around, she found more than a few of the men eyeing her with curiosity. A thin, leather-skinned soldier spat, then asked, "What regiment you with, son?"

"The 2nd Virginia." She hoped no one from her regiment was here. If they recognized her, she'd be exposed as a woman and a traitor.

She patted the lad on the back for reassurance, then approached the Yankee guards. "I'll be needing to speak to one of the wounded men."

The guard sneered, showing brown broken teeth. "A Reb?"

"No, he's one of yours. His name's Alexander Hart."

He scowled. "You're not seeing no wounded men. You're to stay right here where you've been put."

"Could you at least bring me word of Mr. Hart."

"Mister?"

"*Captain* Hart," she corrected. The Union doctor had called him *captain*. "Please, I must see him."

The guard let out a snort. "You're not goin' nowhere, Reb."

The man moved away, laughing with another guard. Katie balled her fists. How was she going to get to Alex?

By the saints, she'd find a way.

****

Alex opened an eye. The scene before him left him dizzy. Doctors, nurses, and stewards bustled between cots set out in rows, taking nearly all the space in the tent.

His first thoughts went to Katie. He'd fallen asleep or passed out—he wasn't sure which—before he could learn if Elliot had found her.

"Did you hear tell of General Reynolds?" a steward asked.

One of the doctors, a thin balding man, looked at the young man expectantly.

"He was killed out in the field. Shot in the neck."

"My God!" the doctor exclaimed.

The doctor moved away, answering the call of another wounded man.

Alex signaled to the younger soldier. "Steward," he rasped.

"Sir?"

"Is the battle over?" He hadn't heard any gunfire since waking and shadows at the tent opening signaled twilight approaching.

"It's done for the day, sir. Our troops are spread out on the high ground."

Alex lay back. A sharp pain shot up his side, drawing a gasp.

"Sir, should I fetch one of the doctors?"

"I'll be fine," Alex said as the pain subsided. "But I would like to speak to Dr. James, if he's about."

"I believe he is, sir. I'll fetch him for you."

Alex took a deep breath, trying not to make any sudden movements. Frantic to learn about Katie, he hoped Elliot had some news. On the far side of the tent, a man screamed and pleaded for the doctors not to take his leg. One of the doctors called for chloroform, and the man quieted.

Alex exhaled and tried to order his thoughts amidst all this chaos. Where was Elliot?

"Are you in pain?" a familiar voice asked.

Alex glanced up into his friend's concerned eyes.

"I'm all right."

Elliot frowned. "You are far from all right, my friend." He checked Alex's bandages. "I don't see any fresh blood, but don't move around too much."

"Have you found Katie?"

"Ah, your lady love." He shook his head. "I'm afraid I've no word of her."

An idea dawned on Alex. "She was in Rebel uniform. Could she be with the prisoners?"

"It's possible. When I have a spare moment, I'll see if I can find out."

Alex lifted his head to glance around the tent. "Looks like you'll be busy for quite awhile. Maybe I could go."

"Absolutely not." Elliot scowled. "If you try to get up, you'll start to bleed again. Allow me to handle this."

"But—"

"Doctor's orders. You are not to move from this spot."

"Doctor," someone called from the back of the tent.

Elliot glared at Alex. "I've got to go. You stay put."

Elliot moved off.

Alex sighed. He'd be damned if he'd just lie here while Katie could be in serious danger. No matter what his friend said, he had to find her as soon as possible.

Lifting his head, he glanced around to make sure no one noticed him. Everyone around him was either occupied or in too much pain to care about him. He gingerly raised himself onto an elbow on his good side. A sharp pain sent him gasping, collapsing flat on his back.

A thin woman with straw-colored hair rushed to his side. "You mustn't try to get up yet," she scolded. She adjusted her spectacles. Leaning over him, she checked his bandages.

Her eyes met his and softened. "Whatever you need, sir, I'll be only too happy to get it for you."

"I need to find a woman. After I was shot, she brought me here. I don't know what's happened to her."

"What's her name?"

"Katie O'Reilly."

"I'll ask the other ladies if they know anyone by that name."

Alex shook his head. "I don't think she'd be with the other ladies in camp. She was dressed in men's clothes...a Rebel uniform."

The woman stiffened. "Dressed as a Reb soldier?"

"She helped me escape from the Rebel camp and brought me here when their pickets shot me. I have to find her." He hoped the desperation in his voice would appeal to her sense of charity.

The woman frowned.

"She may have been put with the Rebel prisoners," he went on. "If you could find her for me, ma'am, I'd be much obliged." He smiled, trying to soften her resolve.

"Ah...I suppose I could ask the guards if they've seen your friend."

"Thank you, ma'am." He sagged against his pillow.

She patted his shoulder. "You just rest and do what the doctor tells you. I'll see about your friend."

Alex sighed, hoping the woman would be able to find Katie.

****

Katie paced restlessly. The men around her sat or lounged on the ground, using their sleeves as pillows. The afternoon heat and humidity threatened to send her into a faint, but she couldn't rest until she learned what had become of Alex.

"Calm yourself, boy," a gray-haired soldier named Zeke said. "No use tuckerin' yourself out." He eyed her with kindly gray eyes.

"I fear fer me friend. He could be dead, and I'd be none the wiser."

"Reckon you can't help him if he's dead."

"But what if he's hurt? He may be calling fer me."

"Son, calm yourself," Zeke repeated. "These bluebellies ain't about to allow the likes of us out of here no how."

Katie wiped the sweat from her brow and sat cross-legged across from him.

"What am I going to do?" She buried her face in her hands.

"Not much you can do, I reckon."

"The guards won't tell me anything." She glared across the pen at them. "We should break out of here. The lot of us."

Zeke guffawed. "And just how do you propose to do that, son?"

She glanced around the pen, her gaze resting on Caleb. The young drummer boy lay stretched out on his back taking a nap.

"I have an idea," she said.

After conferring with Caleb and a few of the other men, Katie formed a plan to distract the guards. When the hot, lazy afternoon erupted into cannon blasts that shook the ground, she knew the time was right.

"Watch me, Caleb," she whispered to the lad. "When I get the guards' attention, you slip out."

Caleb nodded gravely, ready to do his part.

Katie loosened the buttons on her shirt and approached the guards. "Ye've made a mistake," she said.

The men glared at her.

"Get back where you were, Reb," one of them

said.

"I'm a woman. You can't keep me caged up with all these men."

The guard laughed. "That's a new one." He motioned to the other guard. "This here Reb says he's a woman."

The other guard's eyes widened.

Katie smiled. "Come closer, and I'll show you."

Both men seemed intrigued when she loosened more of her buttons. "Have you ever seen these on a man?" She lowered the neckline of her shirt to expose the swell of her breasts. The guards gaped. She hoped Caleb was ready to do his part.

"Well, I'll be," one of the guards said. "Reckon we should get this one out of the pen."

"And do what with her?" the other one asked.

"We'll think of something." The first guard leered.

Katie's heart beat frantically. She waited for the signal.

"C'mon, missy," the first guard said, "I want to feel them to make sure they're real." He reached a beefy hand toward her.

The sound of horses' frantic whinnies distracted everyone.

"What the hell's goin' on?" the second guard asked.

"We'd best go check on it. Most everybody's out on the battlefield." He turned back to Katie. "I'll be right back, missy. Don't you go nowhere."

The commotion of panicked horses and men's shouts told Katie that Caleb had completed his task to sneak into the horse corral, agitate the animals, and free them. After that, she'd told him to run for the woods.

She turned back to the other prisoners. "Come on, 'tis our chance."

The men followed her over the low railing of the

pen and out into the woods surrounding the camp. They raced in all directions. The sounds of battle to the north added to the confusion.

Men's shouts, followed by rifle blasts, scattered the escaped prisoners. One of the men following Katie, screamed as a blast knocked him to the ground. Another man to her left, flew forward, propelled by another gunshot.

Katie's heart hammered. She raced through the woods for her life.

Chapter Seventeen

Katie thought her lungs would burst. Under cover of dense brush, she bent over with hands on knees, panting. Several other soldiers, including Zeke, gathered around her.

Zeke eyed her warily. "You're really a woman?"

"Me name's Katie. I've been with the 2nd Virginia since just after the war started."

Zeke frowned. "The men serving with you don't know you're a woman?"

She shook her head. No use going into a lengthy explanation. "You and the others should skirt around the town and head back to camp."

"You're coming with us," Zeke stated.

She shook her head. "I've something I must do first." In truth, she couldn't go back to the other camp, she'd be taken prisoner. Her only hope was to blend in with the civilians. Maybe then she'd have a chance of finding Alex.

At dusk, Katie and the men still with her crept from the cover of brush where they'd hidden. Caleb had joined them. Since Katie couldn't go back to camp, she made sure Zeke would see him safely there.

At nightfall, they made their move, circling east of town, then started north. Katie said goodbye and continued alone. When she found a stream, she dropped to her knees and splashed water on her face, then cupped her hands and drank her fill.

Once clear of the wooded area, she could distinguish soft light glowing in the windows of a farmhouse.

When she drew nearer, she noticed the darkened barn—the perfect place to rest. Maybe she could sneak into the barn and bed down.

She carefully lifted the latch on the door. Hearing no shouts or movement coming from the house, she slipped into the dark interior. With only the moonlight filtering through the rafters to guide her, Katie felt her way through the barn. The animals paid her no mind. After finding a clean, empty stall, she settled down to sleep.

****

July 3, 1863

Katie woke well before dawn and crept back into the woods to avoid being discovered by the farmer. Concealing herself in the dense brush outside the perimeter of the farm, she tried to decide on her next move.

When dawn approached, she waited, her stomach gnawing with hunger. Where was she to go now? The morning turned bright and sunny. She watched the farmer's wife emerge from the house, carrying a large basket. If she crept up undetected, maybe she could see if the woman had any clothing in the laundry that she could take. She hated to steal, but she had no choice. She couldn't hide in the woods indefinitely, nor could she go around town in her uniform.

She waited for a while, dozing on and off, until she thought it was safe to approach the back of the house. The farmer headed from the barn, whistling when his wife called him to breakfast. Seeing no one else on the premises, she stayed put until he went inside, then made her move.

A brown one-piece dress and calico, cloth bonnet caught her eye. If she could snatch these, she'd be able to enter town as a civilian.

She crept behind the house. Taking the pins from the dress and bonnet, she gathered the bundle against her chest and raced off.

Back in her hiding spot in the brush, she waited, making sure no one had seen her. Satisfied, she moved further into the woods. Once completely out of sight of the farmhouse, she made the sign of the cross and said a "Hail Mary" to beg forgiveness for stealing the clothes. Rolling out her pilfered bundle, she found the clothes only slightly damp. They would dry quickly in the afternoon heat.

After stripping off her uniform, Katie slipped into the gown. Afterward, she rolled her male attire into a bundle, stashing them amid brush. Lifting the bonnet onto her head, she laced it, then started down the road toward Gettysburg.

****

The moans of men in pain roused Alex from sleep. He covered his head with a pillow attempting to silence the noise. Into what depths of hell had he descended? Despite numerous tries to sit up, he fell backwards, his side still plaguing him. Thank God the pain had subsided a bit since yesterday.

The first, familiar face his gaze alighted on was Elliot's. Dark circles lined his friend's brown eyes. He likely hadn't slept at all.

"You look like you should be lying here instead of me," Alex said.

Elliot's lips twitched into a smile that didn't reach his eyes. He peeked under Alex's bandages, nodding approval. "It's healing very well. I'll have the nurse change your bandage."

"I'm on the mend?"

"You certainly are."

"You do excellent work," Alex said.

"No thanks to stubborn patients." Elliot patted Alex's shoulder. "I'm sorry I wasn't able to find your lady friend."

"It's not your fault. One of the nurses told me she'd look for Katie. She had blond hair and spectacles." Alex glanced around the tent. "I don't see her here."

"She should be by soon. I know how worried you are."

Alex studied his friend. "You should get some rest."

Elliot shook his head. "The battle's not yet over. I fear we'll have more casualties today."

As if on cue, a cannon blast sounded, followed by another, then another. Elliot lifted a dark brow. "It's started."

Elliot moved away to prepare for more wounded.

Feeling helpless, Alex sank back against his pillow.

The concussion of cannon blasts reverberated over and over, shaking the ground and sending groans up among the wounded. A nurse approached dispensing water. Alex met her brown eyes behind spectacles and realized this was the nurse who'd promised to get him word of Katie.

"Ma'am." He gripped her wrist to keep her from passing by. "Did you learn anything about my friend?"

"Oh, yes."

Alex's hopes rose. "You found her?"

"Well, no. But I did learn something."

Disappointment sank like a lead ball into the pit of his stomach, but he settled back to hear her account.

"A small group of Rebel prisoners escaped last night. I don't know for sure, but your friend may have been among them."

"With the Rebel prisoners?"

She nodded. "The guards said there was a red-haired woman dressed in men's clothes."

"That would be her." Alex's pulse raced.

"But I'm afraid she's gone with them."

Fearing the answer, Alex asked, "Did they all

get clean away?"

"The pickets shot a few, but most of them disappeared into the woods."

Alex's mouth went dry. *Please, let Katie be with those who'd escaped.*

The nurse patted his hand. "I'm sure your friend's all right."

"If it wouldn't be too much trouble, ma'am, could you find out if the prisoners who were shot were all males?"

She smiled reassuringly. "Of course, sir, I'd be more than happy to."

****

Town of Gettysburg
Afternoon

Rebel soldiers marched through the town while panicked citizens raced in all directions. Cannon blasts shook the ground under Katie's feet and acrid tufts of smoke rose into the sky. She glanced around trying to decide what to do.

A stout woman grabbed her arm. "Ma'am, we need to get out of the street. I'll take you to a safe place."

"But..." Katie's protests went unheeded as several women propelled her to a house on Hanover Street.

Gunshots rang out close by, and a few of the women screamed in terror.

"In here," someone called.

Katie turned. Someone lifted a door in front of the house and exposed a set of stairs leading downward. The group of women pressed around, sweeping her down the stairs into a dank cellar. This must be where they planned to stay until the battle ended.

The last two women in closed the doors, and the small room sank into darkness. Musty scents surrounded them. Bodies pressed around her. She should've run in the other direction. The woman to her left trembled and someone else—likely the home's owner—lit a lantern.

The women—Katie counted eight—herself included, took stock of each other. The gray-haired woman who'd lit the lantern, pointed to a few quilts and blankets for them to sit on, since the small room contained only a few chairs and trunks.

Katie glanced from face to face, sure she'd be exposed as a Rebel and cast out to fare for herself.

The women settled down to wait out the battle. A dark-haired woman sitting beside Katie jumped when a blast shook the floor. "I've never been to a war zone," she said in a nasal, northern accent.

"It will pass," the stout woman said. "We should be quite safe here. You new volunteers will grow used to the hardships in time. If not, you may feel free to return to your homes."

"I don't know if I'll ever grow used to this," a thin, brown-haired woman said.

The stout woman smiled. "I'm sure you'll be fine, dear." Glancing around at the others, she said. "Why don't we pass the time by introducing ourselves? I'll start. I'm Mrs. Harding from Hartford, Connecticut. My husband and two sons serve in the 16th Connecticut Infantry."

"I'm Miss Jackson from Worcester, Massachusetts. My fiancé serves in the 1st Massachusetts Cavalry.

When Katie's turn came, she said, "Me name's Katie O'Reilly. Me husband was killed at Sharpsburg...er, Antietam, last fall."

The women nodded in sympathy.

"What regiment was he with?" the stout woman asked.

"Ah..." Katie hesitated. Would any of these women know what Federal regiments were at Sharpsburg? She took a chance, recalling Alex's regiment. "The 83rd Pennsylvania."

The women nodded their approval. Katie let out the breath she'd been holding. She'd gained the group's confidence. Now, so long as the Yankee soldiers didn't recognize her in her female garb, she'd be able to enter the Federal camp and search for Alex.

****

July 4, 1863

Late in the morning, the group of women volunteers emerged from the cellar to drenching rain.

"It's as if the angels are crying over the deaths of so many brave men," a small, bird-like woman commented.

Katie couldn't help but agree. The townsfolk seemed happy the Union Army had won the battle and the Confederates were heading south, but now they had to deal with what the armies had left behind.

Staying among the group of women Sanitary Commission volunteers, Katie was granted access to the Federal camp. Sure no one would recognize her in women's clothing, she excused herself at the first opportunity and went searching for the 83rd Pennsylvania.

Using her status as a volunteer, she searched the hospital tents but found no sign of Alex. She prayed he hadn't died before she'd gotten to him. A steward told her a few of the local barns were being used to house wounded. Thanking the man, she made her way through drenching rain and found a scene of chaos.

Men moaned and screamed in pain. Blood covered everyone and everything...blankets, pillows, straw spread throughout the barn, aprons of surgeons, as well as women volunteers and rags used to clean wounds. The coppery scent caused

Katie's stomach to clench and blended with the odors of chloroform, alcohol, and sweaty bodies packed so close together. She hated to think of Alex being here.

Making her way gingerly through rows of bodies, Katie reached the back of the barn, hoping to find him.

"Ma'am," a woman called.

Katie turned. A gray-haired woman in a bloody apron held out a ladle. "We could use your help dispensing water to the men."

Nodding, Katie accepted the ladle. She couldn't decline to help, and if Alex were here, she'd eventually find him. She worked her way from man to man and kept hoping the next one would be Alex. At the opposite side of the barn, a chestnut-haired man lying on his stomach turned to face her.

Her breath caught. Although he now had several days' growth of stubble, he was her Alex. She still wasn't used to seeing him without a full beard.

Moving quickly to him, she reached out and stroked his cheek.

****

A cool hand caressed Alex's cheek bringing him out of his dreams. He woke so suddenly, he wasn't sure what he'd been dreaming about. He turned onto his side. Pain shot through his body, wrenching out a groan. A hand stroked his arm, and he gazed up into an angel's face—beneath a dripping wet cloth bonnet—smiling down at him.

"Katie?" he rasped.

"Aye." She smiled, taking his hand.

"How did you...?" He tried to make sense of how and why she'd come to be here.

"I was held with the prisoners," she explained. "That's why I was unable to come to you."

He nodded. "Yes, I heard they had a woman prisoner. You escaped?" His eyes widened when he realized what had happened. "Where did you go, and how did you get back in camp?"

She grinned. "I hid out in a barn, stole these clothes..." She made the sign of the cross over herself. "May God forgive me..."

"And?" He found himself intrigued.

"I went into town and spent the night in a cellar with a group of Northern women volunteers."

"And no one recognized you?"

"In these clothes? No one would ever think to see a soldier dressed like this."

"Fascinating plan," he agreed, "but I fear someone will see through your disguise. You should leave camp immediately."

"How could I not come back? I had to know if you were still alive."

"But I can't protect you now. I nearly died from worry, lying here, unable to look for you."

She pressed her fingers against his lips. Her touch sent a pleasant tingle through his body. Although he worried for her safety, her strength and presence brought comfort. He was glad she'd returned and hoped he'd never lose her again.

****

After Alex had drifted off to sleep, Katie stayed to give assistance to the other wounded men. As the day wore on, her strength began to ebb. She longed for a place where she could sit or even lie down.

"Nurse."

Katie looked up at the tall, dark-haired man who'd called. He motioned to her. He was the surgeon who'd assisted Alex when she'd brought him into camp. Would he recognize her?

"I need some assistance cleaning and bandaging this wound."

"Of course, sir." Katie gazed down at the ugly tear in a young soldier's thigh. She washed out the wound.

The surgeon studied her. "I haven't seen you

before, ma'am. My name is Dr. James."

"Pleased to make yer acquaintance, Doctor. Me name's Mrs. O'Reilly." While she worked, her bonnet slipped from her head, held on by the lacings around her throat.

Dr. James gaped. "*Katie* O'Reilly?"

"Aye."

"Alex's Katie?"

"Aye." Her stomach clenched. Would the man send her back with the prisoners?

"Well, may I say, your new choice of clothing is much more becoming. You looked like a boy the last time I saw you."

Katie flushed, but her heart raced at the fear that he'd turn her in.

"You've nothing to fear from me, ma'am," he said, as if reading her thoughts. "Alex is my friend. He's told me all about you."

Katie smiled, relieved. She finished cleaning out the wound, then wrapped a muslin bandage around the wounded soldier's thigh. "Will Alex be all right? I feared he'd died from the gunshot wound."

"Don't worry yourself, ma'am. He'll be just fine. He needs rest and care." Dr. James smiled. Fine lines crinkled at the corner of his nut-brown eyes. "With you here to care for him, I expect he'll make a full recovery."

Katie completed her task, but when she turned away her vision blurred. She glanced up to clear it, and the room spun.

"Oh, my." She fell to the floor in a dead faint.

Chapter Eighteen

Katie opened her eyes to find Dr. James leaning over her.

"Ma'am, are you all right?" he asked.

"I don't know. I felt dizzy."

The doctor examined her, then helped her to sit up. "I'll get you some water."

She started to protest, but he motioned for her to stay put. He brought her a cup of water, and she downed it greedily.

"Feel better?" he asked.

"Aye."

"Don't fret. I've seen many women—or men for that matter—faint at the sight of wounds and blood."

Katie shook her head. "I've been exposed to much worse, Doctor. I hardly think I'd faint at the sight of blood."

"Well." He patted her hand. "You've been through a great deal. When was the last time you ate?"

She tried to count back but couldn't remember. "I don't recall when I last had anything to eat."

"There you have it." He helped her to her feet. "Doctor's orders are for you to go to the commissary and get yourself some food. I'll take care of Alex until you get back."

"Aye," she said. "Thank you, Doctor." Food in her stomach would feel wonderful.

Katie adjusted her bonnet over her curls before heading out into the rain in search of food. The aroma of ham, potatoes, and corn in the commissary tent set her mouth watering. She marveled at the food available to Union soldiers. She barely noticed the others around her, so focused was she on satisfying her hunger.

After she'd filled her stomach and quenched her thirst with lemonade, she headed back to the barn. On the way, litter bearers continued to bring in more wounded from the field. Since the barn was overfilled with wounded, a tarp had been erected to shelter the new casualties from the rain while they awaited the doctors' attention.

Two of the wounded wore Confederate uniforms. Katie moved close catching sight of one with rust-colored hair and a beard. She sank to the soggy ground when she realized who the man was.

Patrick.

Lifting her apron, she wiped the blood and grime from his face. "Patrick," she crooned. Blood covered his sack coat and trousers. Pulling back the coat flap, she found the wound on his right side.

She'd feared he'd died in the Confederate camp and although relieved to find he still lived, finding him like this broke her heart.

"Oh, Patrick." She pressed her apron to try to staunch the flow.

He stirred and opened his eyes, studying her. "Katie?"

"Yes." She stroked his cheek. A lump rose in her throat.

"The last thing I remember..." He swallowed. "...I was lying on the field. I knew I was killed fer sure and waited for the angels to take me." He grimaced. "Looks like I've found an angel."

"Ye'll be all right. I'll fetch the doctor."

Katie rose, but Patrick's loud moan stopped her. She turned back, unsure of what to do.

"Don't leave me, lass." His handsome features twitched. Katie's stomach clenched. "I'll get the doctor." She turned and hurried into the barn. Dr.

James would help. She prayed he hadn't yet left.

She found him instructing one of the nurses, a young, dark-haired woman, in regards to a patient.

"Dr. James?"

He smiled at her, then frowned. "What is it, Miss O'Reilly?"

The nurse glanced at her, nodded to the doctor, then resumed her duties.

"'Tis me brother-in-law. He's been brought in from the field. Shot."

Dr. James grasped her elbow. "Where is he?"

"Outside. Under the tarp."

"Let's go have a look." The doctor supported her—she didn't think her wobbly legs would hold—and helped her back to Patrick.

James knelt to examine Patrick, talking softly to him. Katie hovered beneath the edge of the tarp to avoid being pelted by rain.

After completing his brief examination, James patted Patrick on the shoulder and rose to face Katie.

"Come with me." He reached for her elbow.

She glanced down at Patrick, who settled back with a grim, resigned expression. The doctor wore the same grim look.

"What is it? Can't you help him, Doctor?"

James didn't answer but motioned for her to go with him. Once they'd returned to the barn, he turned to face her.

"I'm sorry, Miss O'Reilly, but there's nothing I can do for him. His wound is fatal."

Katie's blood turned to ice. "No! There must be something you can do fer him."

James shook his head, dropping his gaze. "As I said, I'm very sorry."

Katie's eyes stung. Her throat grew thick. *Patrick is going to die.*

"I'd like to stay with him, if I could."

"Of course." The doctor squeezed her shoulder. "Take all the time you need."

Katie swallowed past the hard lump in her throat and returned to the tarp. Patrick's eyes were closed, his breathing labored. Sinking to her knees, she stroked his forehead and started the refrain of an Irish lullaby her mother had long ago sung to her.

"The October winds lament across the castle of Dromora..."

Patrick's features relaxed as she sang.

"Sing hush-a-bye lú-ló-lú-ló-lán, Sing hush-a-bye lú-ló-lú." When she finished the tune, his eyes opened.

"Ah, lass, you sing like an angel."

"I have to know. What happened to Bernard?"

"Ah, that." He coughed. "They sent him away to a hospital. I don't know if that bastard is still alive."

"And you?"

"The wound wasn't serious. The doctors fixed me right up. I healed fast enough, and they sent me right back into the fray."

Katie held back a sob. "You didn't get into trouble fer helping us?"

"I told them a Yankee spy sneaked into camp and shot at both me and Bernard."

Katie flushed with anger. "But how could they send you back into the ranks so soon? Ye'd been shot!"

"We're short of men, lass." His gaze seemed to turn inward. "Even more so after this last battle."

Tears spilled down her cheeks. She stroked his face and took his hand.

"I love you, Katie."

"And I love you."

He grimaced. A shudder passed through his body. "I can't be around to protect you as I promised Rory."

"'Tis all right," she whispered.

"Find yer Virginia gentleman and make a life with him. He loves you."

She nodded. "I know he does."

"The war doesn't matter, lass." His gaze seemed to pass through her as if he were focusing on something far beyond her. "Love is all that matters. We were wrong to seek revenge. All of us."

"No. The Yankees have destroyed everything. We were happy until they took it all away."

"Look for..." A gurgling sound silenced him. His eyes glazed over.

Katie tried to rally him, but he shuddered and was gone. "No!" she cried. She made the sign of the cross. Gently, she closed his eyes, then rose and stumbled away.

****

Katie walked, not caring where. Her gown grew sodden. Her actions had betrayed everyone she loved. She'd fallen in love with the enemy, for Alex in his role as a Union spy had aided the Yankees in their pillaging and killing.

She thought of Rory and her baby born dead. If not for the war, they'd be happily living on their Virginia farm. The baby would be two by now, and she'd likely have another on the way.

The Yankees had destroyed everything, and Alex was one of them. How could she be happy with a man who'd, though indirectly, caused the deaths of her family, her life?

She wandered through camp, heedless of the mud. Raindrops sloshed from the brim of her bonnet onto her chin. She longed to lie down and give up. Life was just too hard.

Hours later, thoroughly soaked and exhausted, she wandered into a stable, found an empty stall and curled up, falling into the sleep of the dead.

****

July 5, 1863

Alex woke with a start. Throbbing pain stabbed his side when he moved. He sucked in a breath and glanced about the barn, hoping to see Katie. Lanterns illuminated the large area. Women moved among the wounded men, but none of them Katie. Perhaps she'd gone somewhere to rest.

"Ma'am," Alex said to a young dark-haired woman as she passed between the rows of men. "Is Dr. James still about?"

"Why, yes, I do believe he is, sir. I'll fetch him for you."

Alex settled back to wait. He had to know where Katie was. That she was safe. He couldn't lose her again.

Elliot appeared, his dark hair mussed. "What can I do for you, my friend?" he asked.

"Could you tell me where Katie's gone?"

Elliot shook his head. "I haven't seen her since yesterday."

"Yesterday?" Alex's blood chilled.

"She was tending to a Confederate soldier, said he was her brother-in-law."

"Patrick," Alex said.

"I'm not quite sure what the young man's name was, but he was in a bad way. I fear he's expired."

"And Katie?"

"As I said, I haven't seen her since last night. I do hope she's all right."

"I should have been with her."

"You have problems of your own, my friend." Elliot stared off into space, then patted Alex's shoulder. "I'm sure she's all right. She's likely sleeping off her grief."

"If you see her..." Alex found himself unable to finish what he wanted to say.

Elliot nodded, understanding in his eyes. "I certainly will." He turned away to attend to another patient.

Alex needed to find Katie. If no one else had time to do it for him, he'd have to find her himself.

Grunting, he lifted himself on his elbow on his good side, then slid his feet to the floor. He pushed himself to a standing position. A wave of nausea washed over him. Beads of sweat broke out on his forehead, and the room swayed.

He fell to the floor in a dead faint.

****

Katie stood under the tarp the embalmer had erected. Heavy rain continued to fall. She'd managed to squirrel away some money for emergencies and had contracted with the man to prepare Patrick's body to be shipped back to Virginia. She wanted him to be buried beside his parents and brother.

Although Patrick had encouraged her to stay with Alex, she no longer had the heart for it. Patrick's death had made her all the more determined to seek revenge for her family's sake. Alex no longer fit into her plans. She'd hired a horse and wagon to see Patrick home herself. After that, she'd figure out what to do next.

Mr. Jacobs, the embalmer, a portly, round-faced man with thick spectacles, assured her he'd have Patrick ready for his journey.

"First thing tomorrow mornin', young missy."

Nodding, she turned away only to find herself face-to-face with Dr. James. She jumped back a step in surprise.

"Dr. James!"

He nodded toward the embalmer. The man retreated into his tent. "I see you've made arrangements for your brother-in-law."

"Aye."

"You're having him shipped to his family?"

Katie shook her head. "He's got no one except me. I'll see him home."

"And where is home?" James watched her

closely.

"Virginia. His family owned a small farm there."

He nodded. "Are you returning there to live?"

She shook her head. "There's nothing left to go back to," she said sadly. "'Tis all gone to ruin by now."

"I'm sorry." He stared at the ground as if trying to decide something. "After your relative has been laid to rest, will you return?"

Katie hesitated, not sure what to say.

"The army could use a dedicated nurse like you. And it sounds like you've got little else."

"Aye. But both armies are in need of nurses."

"I understand. After all, you're from Virginia. But so is Alex, and he desperately needs you."

"I fear me loyalties lie with the South, and he's made a different choice."

Dr. James let out his breath in a whoosh. "At least come by the hospital to tell him you're leaving. He's been frantic with worry over you."

"I can't." Katie started to pace. "No. I can't face him again."

"Why not?"

"He'd beg me to stay. And I can't."

"He loves you, Miss O'Reilly."

"'Tis why I can't stay."

James stared at the ground. "You don't love him."

"No. You don't understand. I do love him, but I can't. I can't love the enemy."

"Please reconsider. Your leaving now would wound him even more than his gunshot injury. He's already been left by the woman he'd planned to marry because of war politics. You were helping him heal. Don't do this to him."

Katie looked into the doctor's dark eyes. "Yer a fine friend to Alex. How long have you known him?"

"Since before the war started. We attended

university together in York, Pennsylvania."

She nodded, trying to assuage her guilt at leaving so abruptly.

"At least, tell him you're leaving," James pleaded. "Say goodbye."

Her eyes misted at the thought of Alex waiting for her.

"I can't," she said.

****

Alex's pain had eased somewhat. He sat propped on his cot with a rolled up blanket at his back. He longed to get up and move around, but after he passed out, the nurses had refused his requests to help him stand. They told him the doctor feared he'd reopen his wound.

When Elliot appeared, Alex looked at him hopefully. "Have you found her?"

Elliot nodded, but glanced away.

"Well, where is she?"

"With the embalmer. She's making arrangements to take her brother-in-law's body back to Virginia."

"She's taking the body back herself?" Alex hoped he'd heard wrong.

Elliot nodded. "She said there's no one to ship the body to."

"She'll be coming back afterward, I'm sure."

His friend looked away.

"Tell me! Is she planning to come back?"

"No."

Alex exhaled loudly and rubbed his temple as the twinges of a headache threatened. The woman vexed him. "I have to speak to her. Have her come see me before she leaves."

"I tried to convince her to see you." Elliot eyed him. "She told me she can't."

"What do you mean, she can't?" Alex's blood heated. She couldn't just leave him like this, never to return. "I have to go to her, then."

Elliot raised a finger in warning. "You are not to leave this cot. You're damn lucky you didn't reopen your wound the last time."

"I can do it if you help me."

Elliot shook his head.

"Help me stand, and you can walk me out to her," Alex pleaded. He knew he sounded desperate, but he couldn't let her leave without seeing him.

"Stay put," Elliot ordered. "There's nothing you can do. She's made up her mind."

The calls of another patient led Elliot away.

Alex sank back against his blanket. He didn't care what Elliot said, he had to see her.

Sitting back up, he slowly slid his feet to the floor and gingerly eased himself to standing. So far, so good. A wooden crutch propped against a chair at the entrance of the tent caught his gaze. If he could make it to the crutch, he could get outside.

A backward glance assured him Elliot was occupied, and Alex slowly worked his way to the chair. He kept his breathing slow and steady to ease his lightheadedness. Once he'd made it to the chair, he sat for a moment gathering his strength.

Using the crutch for support, he rose again and took a few tentative steps outside. The July afternoon was overcast and rainy. Alex hesitated, but the thought of never seeing Katie again spurred him on.

He used the crutch to make his way along the muddy ground. The embalmer's tent was usually set up close to the hospital. His labored breath came in gasps, but he refused to turn back.

At the side of the embalmer's tent, a wagon stood with what looked like an enshrouded body in the bed. He heard voices from inside the tent but couldn't make out what they said. He ducked under the edge of the tarp to escape the rain. Katie emerged from the tent followed by a portly man.

The man eyed Alex quizzically.

Katie stared open-mouthed.

"You're all set, young lady." The man glanced at the wagon. "Do you have a horse?"

"Aye, I've hired one. It should be brought around any time now."

The man nodded. "Then Godspeed to you, Miss." Looking at Alex, he asked, "What can I do for you, sir?"

Alex shook his head. "I'm here to see the young lady."

The man nodded. "Then good day to you both." He returned to his tent.

Unable to stand any longer, Alex sank to a stool beside a table set under the tarp.

Katie flinched as if she longed to aid him, but she stood still and watched him. "Why are you here?"

He gazed into her beautiful eyes. "I've come to tell you..." He hesitated, not wanting to sound desperate.

"Tell me what?" She eyed him warily.

He took a deep breath. "Not to go."

Chapter Nineteen

Katie's heart sank as she gazed at Alex. His skin was pale, he wobbled on his feet and seemed to have trouble catching his breath, but he'd never looked more handsome. Yet she couldn't allow him to shake her resolve.

"I'm taking Patrick home. I'm all he's got."

Alex nodded. "Elliot told me. I'm sorry. He was a good man." His knuckles went white on the crutch handle. "I understand your wanting to take him home. Under other circumstances, I'd go with you. But I'd rather you not go alone."

"'Tis no one who can accompany me. Besides, I can very well take care of meself. I've done it before."

He smiled, and it nearly broke her heart.

"I know you can, Katie Rose. But I still fear for you. I want to be at your side. Always."

"I'm sorry, Alex. I have to go." She longed to throw herself into his arms and swear she'd never leave, but her family loyalty wouldn't allow her to do that.

"Very well. Take Patrick home, but tell me when you plan to return."

"I...I wouldn't be knowing."

He tilted his head and studied her as if trying to commit her face to memory. "Don't know when or don't know if?"

Katie shook her head. The man exasperated her. This was why she'd wanted to sneak away. She couldn't face him.

"You told me you had nothing left in Virginia. That's why you'd joined the army alongside your husband. After you tend to Patrick, what on earth will you do?"

"I don't know," she admitted. "I need time alone, to think."

Alex ducked his head. When he looked up, he gazed at her so long, she nearly broke.

"Take all the time you need, Katie Rose." He used the crutch to push himself to his feet.

Glancing down, she noted he was barefoot, his feet mud encrusted. "I wouldn't be thinking the nurses or Dr. James gave you permission to be up and about."

He grinned. "No, ma'am, they didn't."

"Goodbye, Alex."

"Goodbye, Katie Rose...whatever you do, be sure to come back to me."

She turned away, desperately trying to swallow the lump in her throat. As she heard the sloshing, sucking sounds his feet made through the mud, she longed to go after him.

No, don't, or you'll never be able to leave.

****

Fairfax County, Virginia
July 12, 1863

Katie lifted the train of her cloth bonnet to allow the weak breeze to circulate around her neck. The day had started warm and humid and now—early in the afternoon—was heating up into a scorcher. Even the shade of the wide oak she sheltered under didn't help all that much.

She spread the bouquet of bluebells she'd gathered over Rory and the babe's grave sites. Rory's parents rested on his left next to the baby. The right side was reserved for her. On the other side of Rory's parents, Patrick had been put to rest under the newly turned earth. Only she and Father Maguire had been in attendance. Family and friends were either gone, moved on or in the army.

St. Anne's Church, where the cemetery was located, was a tiny structure. Very few Roman Catholics resided in Virginia. Rory's ancestors, who'd come to America over a century ago, had helped to found the church.

As she spread the rest of the flowers over the other graves, Father Maguire asked, "Will you be going back to yer family in New York City, lass?"

She shook her head. "Me brother sent word after I'd joined the army that our parents had died of typhus. Just before the draft riots, me brothers went west to escape serving in the army, and me sister is now married to a man in California. I don't think I could find them while the war's still on, if I wanted to."

"Do you want to?" the priest asked.

"I fear I don't know what I want, Father. Me life's in shambles."

The priest patted her shoulder, his brown eyes kind. "'Tis understandable. Ye've had to bear a great deal." He looked at the ground for a moment as if coming to a decision. "If ye've nowhere else to go, I know of a woman in town who owns a boardinghouse. She could use some extra help. I'm thinking she'd be happy to give you room and board in exchange for some good, honest work."

"Aye, Father, that I could do." Relief washed over her as she realized she now had the time she needed to decide what turn her life would take.

****

Gettysburg, Pennsylvania
Same day

Alex sat with Elliot beneath the spreading shade trees in the Union camp. Although Alex had recovered enough to leave the medical tent, Elliot wouldn't allow him to return to active duty.

The Confederate Army had withdrawn from the area on July Fourth, leaving their dead and seriously wounded men behind. The Union Army and local citizens were left to clean up the mess, while Lee's army had escaped safely to Virginia.

Alex thought of Katie. Somehow, even though he hadn't expected her to return, he'd hoped she loved him enough to come back. But she was gone and though he still worried over her, he could do nothing but go on with his own life.

Elliot sliced off a piece of an apple and offered the slice to Alex. He accepted it and studied his friend. Dark circles smudged his lower lids. His complexion had grown wan and his eyelids drooped.

"You look as though you could use a long furlough," Alex said.

Elliot's lips curved into a smile. "Don't we all."

"The battle's been over for days."

"But the wounded remain." Elliot's expression turned earnest. "Until we can get them all stable and shipped to a military hospital or home, our work is far from finished."

Alex bit into the apple savoring the juicy sweetness. "And when you're finished here?"

"I've orders to return to Washington to work in one of the hospitals there."

Alex smirked. "At least you'll be out of the line of fire." He took another bite. "What about you?"

"I should be heading to Washington myself for further orders."

"And what of you and Mrs. O'Reilly? Is there no hope for reconciliation?" Elliot eyed him.

"I don't believe I'll ever see her again."

"Somehow, I refuse to believe that."

"Why?" Alex wondered what his friend suspected about their relationship.

"There's true love between you. This is nothing like you and Miss Annabelle."

Alex grimaced. "Annabelle's engaged to a

177

Confederate Infantry captain."

"Do tell." Elliot sipped his tea and waited for Alex to continue.

"She visited camp while I was posing as a Rebel soldier in the 2nd Virginia."

"Did she recognize you?"

"Yes, she did."

Elliot frowned. "She didn't turn you in to her intended?"

"No." Alex shrugged. "I'm still not sure why."

Elliot chuckled. "I do believe the lady still carries feelings for you."

Alex scowled.

"Fortunate." Elliot took another sip of his drink. "I hate to think of you wasting away in a Rebel prison or facing execution."

"Can't say I understand women. But I am grateful."

"And her intended?"

"A real bastard. I'd like to think they deserve one another, but even she doesn't deserve that. And the last time I saw him, he'd been shot. Don't know if he survived."

"Well, I'm afraid it's no longer any of your concern, my friend."

Alex nodded.

"But as to Miss Katie..."

"You, sir, are a meddler."

Elliot laughed. "I just happen to think the two of you could work well together."

"A Rebel soldier and a Union spy." Alex shook his head. "You're dreaming, friend."

"Sometimes dreams are all we have."

****

Boardinghouse in Fairfax County, Virginia
October 15, 1863

Katie stood over a basin set on the butcher-block kitchen table, peeling potatoes for tonight's dinner.

Since burying Patrick last July, she'd been living in a small but adequate room in Mrs. Borden's boardinghouse earning her keep by helping with laundry, cooking, and cleaning.

The war was going well for the South. Just a month ago, they'd emerged victorious at Chicamauga. Hearing the accounts of faraway battles left a hollow feeling inside her. She missed the army, the excitement of combat, the camaraderie of the men. She thought about Alex and often reckoned she'd made a mistake, but after all this time, she had no idea where he was and could do nothing about it now.

Although she valued her landlady's friendship, she felt so alone. Rory's family was gone, and what was left of her own, far away. The army had become her whole life.

As she finished with the potatoes, Mrs. Borden entered the kitchen. The woman was short and round, only coming to Katie's chin. The landlady opened the oven and slid a warm loaf of bread onto the cutting board.

Katie's stomach rumbled at the delicious aroma. The blast of heat from the open oven made the already hot kitchen stifling. She wiped a hand over her brow.

Mrs. Borden brushed her plump hands on her apron as she turned to regard Katie, her green eyes sharp in her doughy face.

"I'd say your time here has been good for you, my dear. You were such a pale, scrawny thing when you first arrived. Now, your cheeks have filled out, you have a glow about you and your figure is plumping out nicely."

"There's no dearth of fine food you serve to your guests. With the war going on, how on earth do you do it?"

Mrs. Borden winked. "I have my resources."

Katie raised her eyebrows. "A Yankee supplier?"

"I'll never tell."

Katie laughed, sure her landlady would never associate with Yankees.

Thoughts of Yankees brought Alex to mind. He'd looked so forlorn when she'd last seen him. She couldn't help but wonder where he was and if he still thought about her.

She stoked the stove with more wood and put on a pot of water for the potatoes. The heat rose making it difficult to breathe. She mopped her brow with the hem of her apron, swaying as a wave of dizziness washed over her. Moving away from the stove, she tried to find a chair to rest on.

Before she could reach for it, the room spun, and she fell to the floor in a faint.

****

Military Headquarters in Washington, D.C.
October 20, 1863

Alex paced the hall, waiting to be summoned into the office of Colonel Tinnemann. He'd been given a clean bill of health since suffering the gunshot wound at Gettysburg and was eager to get back to work.

He smiled when he caught sight of Elliot striding down the hall. They shook hands as his friend looked him up and down.

"You're looking quite well," Elliot said.

"Sorry I can't say the same for you." Elliot's complexion was pale, and his face had thinned.

"There's no rest for the weary in the hospitals. We receive more wounded and ill men each day than we release...or lose to death." Elliot frowned.

"Sorry to hear that."

"Well, the Reb victory at Chicamauga didn't help matters. They're still shipping wounded from there."

"Hopefully the tide will turn," Alex said.

"Well said." Elliot smiled. "How goes it with you?

I was hoping you'd stay in Washington. Take an administrative job, perhaps."

Alex shook his head. "No paperwork for me. I was about to request a new assignment in the field."

Elliot scowled. "You've done well above what your county asked of you. I suggest you lay low for awhile."

Alex grinned. "No sir, I need excitement."

"You won't get any in a Reb prison."

"They'd have to catch me first."

"You, my friend, are an adventurer, and I fear it will be the death of you."

Alex laughed.

"On second thought, perhaps there's a certain red-head you're hoping to cross paths with again." Elliot grinned.

Alex shook his head. "I'm afraid that part of my life is over."

Chapter Twenty

*Boardinghouse in Fairfax County, Virginia
December 24, 1863*

Katie hummed "Deck the Halls" as she stood at
the kitchen table preparing cornbread stuffing. Mrs.
Borden was making a Christmas turkey for all her
tenants.

Last October after Katie had fainted, the
landlady had summoned the doctor who'd examined
her and announced that she was in the family way,
about five months along.

She was now in her seventh month with the
impending birth set for February. She'd lied to the
doctor saying the baby belonged to her late husband,
but she couldn't fool Mrs. Borden as easily.

Counting back, Katie realized she'd conceived
when she and Alex had hidden in the cave north of
Chancellorsville after she'd freed him. She told her
landlady the whole story of her adventure with a
Yankee spy. Afterward, Mrs. Borden drew in a deep
breath and tilted her head, studying Katie. She fully
prepared to be ejected from the house.

But her landlady surprised her.

"Your Yankee sounds like an honest, decent
man. And," she added with a twinkle in her eyes,
"I'll bet he's a handsome devil."

Katie flushed and smiled. "Aye. That he is."

"Well then..." Mrs. Borden nodded. "A woman in
love sometimes does things she later regrets but
wouldn't have changed for the world at the time."

Katie prepared to stuff the turkey. The baby

kicked, bringing a smile to her lips. She was carrying Alex's child, and she couldn't be happier.

"I don't regret this." She patted her stomach. "You see, I lost me husband's child, then lost *him* shortly afterward. I look on this as a blessing. A gift from God."

Mrs. Borden nodded. "Now, don't you worry none, dear. I know how to hold my tongue and don't believe in passing judgment on others. 'Judge not lest ye be judged,' the Good Book says." She lifted the lid of the pot to check on the potatoes. "You're welcome to stay just as long as you like. I'm right happy to have you and will welcome the patter of little feet if you choose to stay on."

Warmth spread through Katie at the woman's invitation. She hadn't felt welcome anywhere for such a long time. She'd only had a short time with Rory. After losing him, she'd dreamed of having a family and home again. She swore she'd do better by her own children than what her parents had been able to provide.

With Rory and the farm, she'd had such a chance. But she'd lost that forever. Now, she had a chance to at least start over with Alex's child, even though she was only an employee at the boardinghouse and she didn't have *him*.

As she looked into her landlady's kind eyes, Katie swallowed the lump in her throat. "I'm grateful fer yer offer, Mrs. Borden. 'Tis been a long while since I've had anything to call a home."

"My own grandchildren don't live hereabouts. With the war on, don't reckon I'll get to see them any time soon. It'll be wonderful to have a baby in this house."

Tears welled in Katie's eyes. Even though it was only a room in a boardinghouse, she felt like she'd finally found a home.

Once the turkey was in the oven, the women sat

at the table slicing carrots and radishes Mrs. Borden had stored in her spring room.

"I don't mean to pry," the landlady said, "but when the war is over, will you search for your child's father?"

Katie stared at the knife in her hand and bit her lip. She met the older woman's gaze. "I honestly don't know."

****

Washington, DC
Same day

After a servant divested him of his greatcoat, Alex adjusted his uniform. He'd accompanied Elliot, at his insistence, to a Christmas party at the home of one of the older surgeons.

The sight of ladies in colorful gowns and the sound of laughter and clinking glasses seemed foreign to Alex. The last such party he'd attended had been at his father's mansion before the war to celebrate his and Annabelle's engagement.

He had the urge to bolt, but Elliot caught his arm and guided him into the ballroom. Ladies turned their heads and eyed the two men decked out in their uniforms. Alex bristled, feeling he was on display.

"Come, Alex," Elliot urged. "There are some people I'd like you to meet."

Elliot introduced him to Doctor Chadwick, their host, his wife, Margaret, and daughter, Catherine.

Catherine turned grey eyes, so like Katie's, on him. A lump formed in Alex's throat as he gazed at her flame red hair, arranged in upswept curls, reminding him of what he'd lost.

When the doctors launched into a discussion of field medical procedures, Mrs. Chadwick excused herself to tend to the other guests.

Catherine sighed, glancing sidelong at Alex. "Captain, why don't we leave the doctors to their medical talk and find some refreshments?"

"Thank you, Miss Chadwick."

Alex glanced over his shoulder. So engrossed was Elliot in his conversation, he didn't notice his friend leave.

At the table, Catherine extended a crystal glass to Alex. He helped himself to punch, then filled her glass as well.

Sipping the sweet drink, he turned from the table to watch the couples dancing. A lively reel played, and the dancers swirled about the floor with the ladies' gowns circling around them. His thoughts weren't with the dancers or the ornately decorated hall, but with Katie, the last time he'd seen her in Gettysburg.

"Captain, forgive me for being forward, but you seem a bit sad."

Alex glanced down at Miss Chadwick's upturned face. Any other time in his life, he may have been interested in the young lady, but now his heart belonged to Katie.

"I'm sure you miss your family and home during the holidays."

"I fear I'm no longer welcome in my home."

"That's heartbreaking. Where are you from, Captain?"

"My family lives in Virginia."

"I thought I detected a Southern accent." She tilted her head to study him. "If you're a Southerner, why do you fight for the Union?"

Alex grimaced. "I can't abide seeing human beings treated like animals."

"Bravo, Captain."

Once they'd finished their drinks, they set their empty glasses on the table.

"Captain, I'd like to introduce you to a few friends."

Alex escorted Miss Chadwick over to a group of

guests.

As she made introductions, names and faces blurred in his mind.

All he could think about was Katie and how she'd torn his heart out when she'd left him.

Chapter Twenty-One

Boardinghouse in Virginia
February 14, 1864

The doctor Mrs. Borden had summoned to attend Katie, handed her the small, warm bundle wrapped tightly in a blanket. When she gazed into the baby's blue eyes, she quickly forgot the pain of childbirth.

"Meet your new daughter, Mrs. O'Reilly." The doctor's doughy face turned bright pink as he beamed.

"A girl?" Katie cradled the child against her breast.

Mrs. Borden clasped her hands. "Yes, a beautiful little girl. Isn't it wonderful?"

Katie gazed in awe at the searching eyes and tiny rosebud mouth making sucking motions. "What do I do now?"

Her landlady and the doctor exchanged amused glances. "Here, dear, I'll help you," Mrs. Borden said.

As the doctor busied himself gathering up his instruments, Mrs. Borden approached the bed, cooing at the baby. Rearranging Katie's gown to expose a breast, she guided the child's mouth to the nipple. When the baby latched on, Katie laughed.

"Don't you worry, dear. She knows what to do." Mrs. Borden winked. "If you need any help, just holler. I had four sons and two daughters. I've got loads of experience."

Finished with his task, the doctor turned to her. "I'll leave you in the capable hands of Mrs. Borden and be by to see you and the little miss tomorrow."

"Thank you, Doctor." Katie couldn't take her eyes from the child suckling at her breast.

She'd dreamed of this day for so long but hadn't thought it possible to experience such happiness.

Mrs. Borden left with the doctor to see him out.

Katie languidly stroked the reddish, downy hair on the baby's head. Her thoughts drifted to Alex. Was he still recovering from his wounds, or had he returned to his spying?

She sighed and cuddled the child. "I don't know where yer da is, little one." The wide blue eyes regarded her with a frown. "I'm thinking after this war is over, we can try to find him. I don't doubt he'll fall madly in love with you..." Her throat closed up, and she wondered if she'd ever see him again.

When Mrs. Borden returned, the baby had drifted off to sleep.

"I'll take her off your hands for a bit, so you can get some rest." The landlady reached to take the child. "Have you thought of a name for her yet?"

Katie nodded. "Aye. Me da used to tell me wonderful stories of a princess in a far off land." She studied the baby in her arms. "I'm naming her Isabel."

****

Culpepper County, Virginia
May 30, 1864

Alex tucked his notepad into his pack and set his brown bowler on his head. He was in the camp of the 8th Virginia regiment posing as a reporter.

Battles had waged for weeks in central Virginia. The locals called the area *The Wilderness*. Soldiers fought in the wild, wooded area amidst dry brush. The resulting fires caused many casualties. Wounded were brought in badly burned, while others unable to get away died awaiting help.

The worst part for Alex was the stench of

charred flesh and the screams of men set afire from blasts of shelling and gunfire.

At midday, he perched on a boulder behind the Confederate lines to observe what he could of the battle being fought in the woods. Pad and pencil in hand, he recorded what he saw and heard.

The stirring sounds of "Dixie" and the tattoo of drums beat out a march to spur the troops onward. Shouts of officers sounded from the woods, mingled with the blasts of rifle fire and boom of cannon. The pungent scent of gunpowder and the brush and trees burning stung Alex's nostrils. Before long, heart-rending screams rose from the shelter of the woods as men were shot down or burned. Black smoke rose above the tree line. How terrifying it would be to be caught in the conflagration.

He paused in his note taking as a plaintive voice—close to the edge of the wooded area—rose above the noise of battle.

"Please, God, help me! I don't want to burn."

Alex placed his pad and pencil beside him and approached the woods. A wave of heat rose like a wall, threatening to send him back. Unable to ignore the cry of the man who seemed to be just a few yards from him, he pulled a handkerchief from his vest pocket, covered his nose and mouth and stepped beyond the trees. Frantically, he glanced around. The smoke made it nearly impossible to see what was directly in front of him.

"Where are you?" he called. "I'll get you out."

"Here, sir," the voice rasped.

Looking down, Alex saw a brogan, then a leg clothed in filthy butternut trousers. He stooped and moved his hand up the leg until he reached the upper half of the man's body. He leaned close to be sure he was the one who'd spoken. No sense risking his life to rescue a corpse. Through the haze, he made out a thin, heavily-bearded face, the skin blackened, eyelids squeezed shut.

Alex leaned close to the man's ear, keeping his handkerchief over his mouth. "Are you still with me, sir?"

The eyes popped open, followed by a racking cough. "I been kilt," the soldier rasped. "But I don't want to burn."

Peering through the smoke, Alex could see the bright red stain spread over the man's sack coat.

"I won't allow you to burn. I'll pull you out."

Stuffing his handkerchief in his pocket, he reached for the man's hands, lifting his arms. He'd drag him out of the woods if he had to. He blinked rapidly trying to reduce the sting. His throat burned as did his lungs, making it difficult to breathe, but he'd promised this man he'd get him to safety.

Yanking on the soldier's arms, he backed in what he hoped was the right direction. He moved around trees and over brush, struggling to breathe, fearing he'd pass out.

Something grasped his ankle, nearly causing him to stumble atop the man he was helping. He peered down and realized another soldier lay beneath him, this one garbed in Union blue.

"Please, help me, sir," he said.

Holy hell! Without letting go of the first soldier, Alex promised, "I'll be right back for you."

"Please, sir..." The man tried to grab Alex's leg again, but he was able to slip his grasp, pulling his charge until he reached the tree line. He let the man's arms drop, then bent over bracing himself with his hands on his knees. Sweat poured off his body, and he doubted he had the strength to continue. But he couldn't leave this soldier lying so close to the woods. No telling how far the fire would spread. He had to get him across the field to the boulders.

Alex stooped and grasped the man under the

armpits. He'd drag him to safety then go back for the Union soldier if he could find him. The Rebel soldier grimaced and let out a feeble yelp as Alex half lifted him and backed away.

From the corner of his gaze, Alex caught movement. A lone Confederate soldier carrying canteens raced toward the woods.

"Private," Alex rasped. "This soldier needs help."

The private approached, seemingly confused by Alex's civilian attire.

He pointed to the soldier at his feet. "He's been wounded. See to him. I have to go back for another man."

While the private attended to the wounded man, Alex poured water from his canteen onto his handkerchief, held it over his nose and mouth, and raced back into the woods.

Locating the Union soldier, he helped him to safety, then returned to took for more wounded.

He didn't care for which side they fought. He refused to leave helpless men to burn.

The black smoke grew thick, and he could no longer see anything. He completely lost his orientation and didn't know which direction would lead him out.

He couldn't see, couldn't breathe. His lungs felt about to burst. Dropping to his knees, he collapsed.

Chapter Twenty-Two

Virginia boardinghouse
July 4, 1864

Katie sat on the porch, bouncing Isabel on her knee as she waved a hand fan trying to stir up a breeze for her and the baby. Assorted pots of colorful blooms as well as window boxes filled with summer flowers adorned the wide porch.

Five-month-old Isabel cooed and waved her chubby arms. Katie kept the baby with her as much as she could, tying Isabel to her back or hip while she did chores.

While the war still raged on, the battles now called 'The Wilderness' and 'Cold Harbor' had ended the fighting in the northern and central areas of Virginia. The latest battle in the eastern front was being waged far south in Petersburg.

Mrs. Borden emerged from the house with two glasses of lemonade. She set one on the wide porch railing and handed the other to Katie. The landlady reached for Isabel and hefted her into her arms.

"And how's my little angel today," she said as Isabel laughed.

"Yer spoiling her, you are," Katie said.

With one arm holding the squirming Isabel, Mrs. Borden placed her other hand on her ample hip. "I need someone to spoil, now don't I?"

Isabel giggled.

The landlady peered and pointed down the road. "Looks like soldiers approaching."

Katie stiffened, her heartbeat speeding up.

"Ours or Yankees."

Mrs. Borden shaded her eyes, then smiled. Katie rose to stand beside her.

"I see the 'Stars and Bars'," Mrs. Borden said.

Katie blew out a sigh of relief when she recognized the Confederate flag.

Mrs. Borden handed Isabel back. "I'd best go make up some fresh lemonade for our brave boys."

The landlady retreated into the house. Katie stood watching the line of soldiers approach. They appeared to be a single company. Where was the rest of the regiment?

The sight of the soldiers stirred feelings in Katie she'd tried to repress. She thought of Rory and Patrick, now lying side by side in the church cemetery. And she thought of Alex. Although she loved living here with Mrs. Borden and Isabel, she missed being in the army. Despite the hardships, she felt a sense of purpose, of being part of something important.

Katie planted a kiss on Isabel's downy cheek. "Ye're me purpose in life now, little one. I'd die before I allowed anything happen to you."

Isabel cooed in response.

When the soldiers neared, Mrs. Borden reappeared with a bucket and ladle. She placed it beside the railing just at the edge of the steps, then waved her handkerchief at the men.

Once they were within earshot, she called, "Got some fresh made lemonade here for our brave fighting men."

The men approached, removing their hats and politely extending their tin cups to accept the offering. Mrs. Borden invited a captain and two lieutenants to have seats on the porch while the rest of the men spread out on the garden grass.

"Much obliged, ma'am." The captain accepted a second cup.

Katie froze and wrapped a protective arm around Isabel. Although thinner, with dirt covering his face like the men under him, she recognized Captain Gerard and feared he'd remember her.

After taking a sip from his cup, Gerard eyed Katie and Isabel. "Beautiful child you have there, ma'am."

"Thank you, Captain. Her name's Isabel."

"Beautiful name. Beautiful." He held Katie's gaze for a moment, a frown creasing his face.

"Where are you all headed, Captain?" Mrs. Borden asked. "We heard the fighting had moved south to Petersburg."

"Yes, ma'am. We've just come from there." He glanced at one of his lieutenants. "We've been sent on patrol to look for deserters."

The landlady gasped. "Deserters around here?"

"Afraid so, ma'am. Most of them are just trying to make their way back home. You haven't seen any bedraggled soldiers hereabout, have you?"

"No, sir," Mrs. Borden said.

He turned to Katie. "How about you, ma'am?"

Katie's blood chilled. She felt sure he'd recognized her. "I've seen no soldiers fer quite a while, Captain."

"Then we'll be moving on, ladies." He moved to retrieve his cap.

Katie held her sigh of relief.

"Before you go, sir," Mrs. Borden said, "could you tell us how things are going in Petersburg?"

Bernard twisted his cap in his hands. "Our boys, as well as the town, are surrounded. We're unable to get supplies in to them. I fear we may be unable to prevail." Looking from Mrs. Borden to Katie, he continued, "I'm sorry to have to tell you this. Is the child's father...?"

Katie shook her head. "He was killed in the fighting long before she was born."

"I'm sorry, ma'am."

She nodded but felt thankful he hadn't recognized her.

****

Union camp near Cold Harbor, Virginia
July 4, 1864

Alex grimaced when his shirt rubbed against the newly acquired scars on his arms and chest. Since rescuing the soldiers in the Wilderness battle last May, he'd been recuperating in a field hospital. The doctor had wanted to send him to a hospital in Washington to recover fully from his burns, but Alex refused. He was not about to waste more time. Alex felt certain Elliot had guessed the real motive for his refusal to leave was to find Katie. He needed to know she was all right. But it would be a nearly impossible task. She could be anywhere.

Against doctor's orders, Alex decided a short jaunt into town would do him good. He needed to stretch his legs, and with no pressing duties, he felt cooped up. In his role as a spy, he'd grown used to sneaking in and out of places right under the enemy's nose. And he could blend in easily with the locals.

Dressed in civilian garb, he reined in his horse at the mercantile of the nearest town of Culpepper to check out the wares. An ample-bodied, blond woman stood behind the counter conversing with a thin, dark-haired woman.

As he inspected a cornboiler, the chatter of the ladies caught his attention.

"She has a young Irishwoman workin' for her. She's a widow with a sweet little baby daughter."

"Why, Mrs. Borden has always been takin' in strays as long as my family's known her."

"Pardon me, ladies," Alex said, "and forgive me for eavesdropping, but did you say a young Irish widow?"

"Why, yes sir," the ample-figured woman drawled. "Do you know her?"

"Can't say for sure, ma'am, but I'm looking for someone who fits that description. Name's Katie O'Reilly."

The blond woman glanced at the thin lady, who nodded. "Yes, sir, I do believe that is her name."

"And you say she has a child?"

"Yes, sir, she's about five or six months old. Pretty little thing."

"A girl?" Alex's blood heated. Katie had apparently left him for good and moved on to another man.

"Yes, she told me the child was her late husband's. He was killed in battle."

Counting back, Alex realized Katie was lying. The child couldn't possibly be her late husband's. But then he recalled the night he and Katie had spent in the cave.

Could the child be his?

"Pardon me, ladies." He left the mercantile and stood outside gulping fresh air.

So, Katie was in town, and she had a child. He'd just have to pay her a visit.

****

Maurice held the dispatch his aide had brought him up to the oil lantern to try to decipher his orders. His men had rounded up three deserters today and upon Maurice's orders, shot them. He didn't want prisoners to slow his men down, and cowards who deserted their posts didn't deserve to live anyway.

Voices outside his tent distracted him. Lieutenant Jenkins and one of the corporals discussed the lemon cookies the woman at the boardinghouse had given them.

"Captain?" Jenkins asked. "Would you care for some cookies?"

"No, thank you, Lieutenant."

"Good night then, sir."

The men ambled off to their tents. The discussion about the boardinghouse brought to mind the young Irishwoman and her child. Something about her seemed familiar. Maurice tried to recall if he'd ever seen her. The image of a thin boy-shaped woman in uniform with short red curls popped into his mind. Although the woman at the boardinghouse wore a dress, had longer hair and a fuller figure, he was certain she was one and the same. The woman who'd allowed Alexander Hart to escape his grasp.

Since he and his men had been ordered to remain in the area, he'd have to pay another visit to that boardinghouse to have a conversation with Katie O'Reilly.

****

Katie stopped to wipe her brow with the edge of her apron as she mashed a pot of potatoes for the noon meal. Sarah, one of the borders who worked in town as a schoolmarm, was entertaining Isabel today. Katie felt grateful for all the help Mrs. Borden and the other tenants gave her. They all adored Isabel, and she thrived on the attention.

Mrs. Borden swept in with a stack of serving bowls she set on the table.

"I'll start taking food to our guests while you finish up here." After filling two bowls with vegetables, she lifted one in each hand and headed for the door. Stopping a moment, she said over her shoulder, "There's a very handsome gentleman outside asking questions about you."

Before Katie could respond, Mrs. Borden had gone through the swinging door.

Katie's pulse raced. Why would a man be asking about her? Both intrigued and worried, she tried to come up with a way to see the man without him seeing her.

Mrs. Borden returned, and they dished the remaining food into the bowls. She scooped up the dishes. "I invited your young man to eat with us."

"Me young man? Why in heaven's name do you assume he's me young man? I don't even know who he is."

"Well dear, if he's not your young man, he sure oughta be." Mrs. Borden pushed ahead into the dining room, leaving Katie no choice but to follow.

She took a deep breath, heart thudding, and braced herself for whoever sat at the dining table.

When her landlady moved to the side of the table, Katie nearly dropped the bowls. Alex Hart gazed up at her. He'd been seated amongst the borders. His lips curved into a smile.

"It's a pleasure to see you again, Mrs. O'Reilly," he said.

Turning toward Katie, Mrs. Borden winked before taking her seat at the head of the table.

Flabbergasted, Katie set her bowls down and swallowed.

"Allow me, ma'am." Alex rose, moved to her side, and pulled out the chair for her.

She shakily slid down, too stunned to speak.

Alex regained his seat across from her and smiled. "Reckon you'd like to know how I found you."

Katie glanced around the table at the other guests, who eyed them with open curiosity. She tried to stay calm. She'd thought Alex to be out of her life forever, and now, here he was. She needed time to sort things out and another thought occurred to her. Did she want him to know about Isabel?

****

All through the noon meal, Alex found himself unable to take his eyes from Katie. Her hair had grown out some, and she now wore it pulled back into a respectable bun, although a few curls escaped at the sides, hanging in fiery tendrils in front of each ear.

She'd also filled out a bit, pleasingly so. That and the simple dress she wore made her utterly appealing. He longed to gather her into his arms and kiss her senseless.

She kept her conversation reticent as if she wanted the other diners to believe the two to be just passing acquaintances. She'd obviously never expected to see him again.

After the meal, she begged off, claiming to have work to do in the kitchen. So, he waited—at Mrs. Borden's invitation—on the porch, settling in the rocking chair. When Katie finally emerged, he rose and rounded on her.

Gently taking her by the elbow, he guided her into the seat he'd just vacated. She sat stiffly, staring at him, her eyes wide. Scraping a straight-legged chair across the porch, he set it directly in front of her.

"Is there something you'd like to tell me, Katie?"

She licked her lips, then glanced down and regarded her hands folded on her lap. "I left after Patrick died because I could no longer aid the enemy."

"The enemy?" Alex stared at her. "You mean me?"

"I understand why you had to do what you did. But I have me reasons for hating Yankees. I can't just change me way of thinking because..." She stopped and lifted her gaze to him.

"Because you love me?" he finished for her.

Her face crumpled. "I can't betray me family."

"Like I betrayed mine?"

She shook her head. "I'm not saying that."

He clenched his fists. "But that's what you think, isn't it?"

"No." She reached for his hand. "I understand why you feel the way you do. I'll not be passing judgment."

"But do you still love me?" he persisted.

"I..."

Mrs. Borden emerged from the house, a child straddled across her hip. "I reckon she needs her mama."

Alex stared at the pink-cheeked baby. She was garbed in a long white gown with a cap covering her hair, but a few wisps of fire-red hair escaped. Katie reached up. The landlady settled the child on her lap.

"Her name is Isabel," Katie said.

Alex felt as if he'd had the wind knocked out of him. He studied the child. Large cornflower blue eyes regarded him. "She's...she's..."

"She's mine."

"Who..." He stopped as he realized Mrs. Borden stood by the door.

Katie cast him a warning glance.

"Would you care for some cookies?" the landlady asked. "I have a fresh batch in the kitchen."

Alex was about to decline when Katie said, "Yes, that would be lovely. Thank you."

Once the woman disappeared into the house, Katie said softly, "I told Mrs. Borden she's me late husband's."

"But that's not possible."

"Aye. But no one here knows when Rory died."

He nodded. Of course she'd need a story like that to keep herself respectable. "But really...is she..."

Katie's eyes widened. "Yer asking if she's yours?"

"Yes, when we were together that last time. In the cave."

Katie swallowed, then set her jaw, her eyes growing cold.

"No, she's not yours."

Letting out the breath he was holding, he realized he'd wanted her to say yes. A small chubby hand reached out to him, grasping at his collar.

Mrs. Borden reappeared with a tray of lemon cookies. After handing one to Isabel, she set the tray on the railing then said, "I'm brewing some fresh tea if you'd like some."

"Please," Katie said, nodding.

Once the woman had left again, Alex stood. He needed a straight answer to ease his suspicion that Katie was lying about the child not being his.

"Who's her father?" he asked.

"No one you know. 'Tis someone I met in passing."

"Before or after you left me."

"'Tis none of yer concern." Katie eyed him coldly.

A lump rose in his throat, and his jaw clenched until it ached. "Reckon I'll be taking my leave then. Send my apologies to Mrs. Borden."

Turning, he stomped down the steps to his horse. Without looking back, he mounted and left. He decided it was high time he forgot Katie O'Reilly. She meant nothing to him now.

Chapter Twenty-Three

Katie descended the stairs after she'd put Isabel down for her nap. Her fingers trembled on the banister, and her face burned with shame. How could she have lied to Alex? She had a sudden urge to barrel down the stairs and race down the road to try to catch him.

A male voice in the entrance hall halted her. Had Alex returned, or was it one of the male borders?

She continued down, then stopped again when she caught sight of a man in Confederate uniform. Captain Bernard stood at the door conversing with Mrs. Borden.

"Why, yes ma'am. I surely would enjoy another cup of your fine lemonade."

Katie debated turning back and creeping to her room, but he'd obviously heard her on the stairs. He looked up and smiled.

"Why, just the lady I've come to see." He motioned for her to descend. "Ma'am, I would like to have a word with you, if I may?"

She clenched her hand on the railing, wondering what the bastard wanted now.

"Please," Mrs. Borden said, "make yourselves comfortable on the porch while I fetch refreshments." She hustled off to the kitchen.

Katie swallowed. She had no choice but to join Bernard. He held the door and motioned for her to precede him. She took a seat in one of the rocking chairs, and he sat on a bench across from her.

Thankfully, before he could say anything, Mrs.

Borden reappeared with a tray containing a pitcher of lemonade, three glasses, and peanut butter cookies.

Katie watched Bernard warily, sure he'd recognized her after he'd left and had returned to take her prisoner.

"If you would be so kind, ma'am," Bernard said to Mrs. Borden, "I'd like to have a word with the young lady here in private."

The landlady frowned. "Begging your pardon, Captain, but you've just met my housekeeper. It doesn't seem proper."

"Quite the contrary, ma'am. We've met before and know each other quite well." He nodded toward Katie. "I just hadn't recognized Miss O'Reilly."

"'Tis Mrs. O'Reilly," Katie hissed.

"Of course. My pardon." Bernard smiled.

Mrs. Borden rose and touched Katie's shoulder. "Is it all right, dear?"

Katie nodded. "I'll be fine."

"I'll be right inside if you need me. Just give a yell." With a final glare in Bernard's direction, she went into the house.

Katie watched Bernard, tension building. "And what is it yer wanting? Have you come to take me away in chains?"

He shook his head. "That wouldn't serve my purpose. All I really want is Alexander Hart. Where is he?"

"I wouldn't be knowing that. I haven't seen him since last summer at Gettysburg."

Bernard smirked. "Any woman who can pass as a man in an army camp for as long as you did has to be an expert liar, don't you agree?"

Katie leaned forward, her fingers clutching the arms of the rocker. "'Tis the truth. The last time I saw Mr. Hart was when I left camp at Gettysburg to transport me brother-in-law's body home for burial. I never saw him again."

"That little girl of yours—" Bernard scratched his chin. "—where's her father?"

"He's dead."

Bernard shook his head. "No, ma'am. I do believe that's Alexander Hart's child."

Katie rose. "How dare you insult me, Captain! Take yer leave now."

"Yes ma'am. I'll do that." Bernard rose and moved so close she felt his breath on her cheek. "But I would keep a sharp eye on that little girl. You wouldn't want any harm to come to her."

Katie gasped. "You bastard! Ye'd sink so low to harm an innocent babe?"

"If it gets me what I want, ma'am." He tipped his hat and descended the porch steps.

Katie's blood boiled as she watched him mount up and ride away. If he so much as touched a single hair on Isabel's head, she'd kill him.

****

Tavern Outside Culpepper
Midday

Alex slouched at a small table in the corner doodling on his notepad. The lunch customers had long gone. A dark-haired barmaid approached.

"Will you be needing anything else, sir?"

He looked up and took in her curvaceous form, then moved to her face. Her pert nose and gray eyes reminded him of Katie. The still raw pain of her betrayal, stabbed at him again.

"No ma'am," he said. "I'm just fine here."

She nodded and retreated to the kitchen.

He took a sip of his lager and thought of the child. He'd wanted her to be his. He'd been alone so long, the idea of Katie as his wife and a beautiful daughter, as well as more children to follow, appealed to him.

But she was just like Annabelle, moving onto

another man when things didn't go her way. He wondered if she was still with Bernard. They may already have married by now.

The tavern, in mid-afternoon, was empty of customers. Alex sat alone. He didn't notice the bartender until the tall, lanky man stood beside his table.

"Is there a problem?" Alex asked.

"No, sir. I just thought you seemed troubled."

Alex smirked. "Troubled is a delicate way of putting it." He motioned to the man. "Have a seat. I can see you've got time to spare."

The bartender pulled out a chair. He extended a hand. "Name's Charles Hoffnagle."

Alex took the man's hand and shook it. "Alex Hart."

Charles nodded and glanced at the notepad. "I've seen you around town. You're a reporter?"

"From *The Richmond Dispatch*. I'm covering the battles hereabouts."

Charles whistled. "Those Wilderness battles have been somethin' fierce and too close for comfort."

Alex nodded. "The fires..." He broke off recalling the screams of men burning and stench of charred flesh.

"You were there?"

"Writing a feature for the paper..."

A clamor of horses outside distracted Alex.

The bartender glanced toward the front windows. "Reckon I'd best get back to the bar. Keep up the good work, sir." He sauntered back to his station.

Alex watched the door, wary of who might enter. He shifted his chair, trying to hide in the shadow of the corner and hoped the new customers wouldn't notice him.

Men's laughter preceded the door opening wide. Alex hunched over his notepad pretending absorption with what was on the page but kept his gaze riveted on the door.

Two Confederate lieutenants entered. Hardly glancing at Alex, they strode to the bar. Another officer followed. Alex wished he could tuck himself into the wall behind him when he recognized Captain Bernard.

Damnation! He'd hoped the bastard had been shot dead.

Bernard followed the others to the bar. Alex dropped a few coins onto the table, gathered his things, and sprinted to the door, hoping the soldiers wouldn't take notice.

Once outside, he swore. He found a bench around the side of the tavern, pulled his hat brim low, and waited. As long as no one recognized him, he'd just hang around to see if he could learn anything new.

A short time later, he heard the men clamor down the steps but stayed put.

"Where to now, sir?" one of the men asked.

"You two are going back to camp," Bernard said. "I'll be paying another visit to that boardinghouse."

One of the men laughed. "Is it those cookies you're sweet on, sir? Or that little Irish lass with the baby?"

Bernard chortled. "Let's just say, I've got some business to discuss with the lady."

Alex didn't move until he heard the men saddle up and canter off. A knot of fear tightened in his chest. As much as he didn't want to face Bernard or Katie again, he had to go back to be sure Katie and her baby were safe.

****

Katie refused to allow Isabel out of her sight, even when Mrs. Borden had offered to spell her. She'd never forgive herself if that bastard got a hold of her child. She kept Isabel by her side bundled in a wicker basket on the back stoop while she washed bed sheets, then moved the basket to the clothesline so she could hang the sheets to dry.

Fear constricted her lungs as she imagined Bernard harming her daughter. She could face any danger herself but couldn't bear this. And no matter her feelings regarding Alex, she refused to betray him. What was she to do?

Before she hung the final sheet, she glanced at the basket. Isabel gurgled raising her tiny, pink fists at the clear, blue sky. Katie smiled. "Be just a minute more, sweetheart." She turned back to her task of spreading the last sheet on the line for pinning.

A prickle shot up her spine. Someone was behind her. She spun and gasped.

Bernard held Isabel in his arms.

Katie's mouth went dry.

Bernard smiled. "What a sweet, little child."

Isabel frowned up at him.

"Give her back," Katie demanded.

"Of course I will. I'd hate to separate a child from her mother."

Katie took a step forward.

Bernard shifted Isabel to one arm and held up his free hand. "Not so fast. I need to know where that traitor Alexander Hart is before I release her."

Heat rose to Katie's cheeks. "You bastard! I told you I don't know where he is."

"You're lying. Trying to protect the child's father, no doubt." He scowled.

"He's not her father." She longed to run and yank Isabel from his arms but feared he'd hurt her.

"Ah, yes. I don't quite believe that story. I think if I take this child, he'll be the one to come looking for her."

"You devil! You'll never take her so long as I'm alive. Why do you want Alex so much anyway?"

"He's a Yankee, a betrayer of his own people and..." He hesitated.

He had to be holding something back. "And what?"

"That's none of your concern, missy. Just tell me what I want to know."

"I can't tell you where Alex is, because I don't know."

Isabel whimpered, then broke into a full-fledged howl.

"Shh." Bernard tried to hush her, then shook her causing her to wail louder. "How do you get her to quiet down?"

Katie raised her arms. "Give her to me."

Bernard frowned, his face turning a bright pink.

"I'll quiet her," she said.

He backed away from her as Isabel's cries rose to a high pitch.

Katie's heart clenched. She couldn't allow him to take Isabel. She'd die first.

She gathered her skirts, preparing to sprint to Isabel's side when a baritone voice behind her stopped her.

"Give the lady her baby."

Katie turned and gazed into Alex's blue eyes. When had he appeared? She hadn't heard him approach.

Bernard smiled. "Just the man I want to see." He held the screaming baby out. "Here, take her."

Katie raced forward and gathered Isabel in her arms. The baby sniffled but quieted as Katie rocked her.

"Go inside, Katie," Alex said.

Her startled glance went from him to Bernard. "But..."

"Do as I say. Get Isabel safe. I'll take care of Bernard."

She nodded. Her skin grew clammy as she

ascended the porch steps. She feared whatever was about to happen, but especially she feared for Alex's life.

****

Alex watched Katie go to the door. Her landlady peered out, a frown knitting her brow. Katie whispered something to her, and both women retreated inside. He turned back to Bernard whose smile turned calculating.

Alex threw open his arms. "What can I do for you, Bernard?"

"You know what I want." Bernard sneered. "I want to see you sent to prison or hanged for your treason."

"Well, now you have me."

"Not so fast." Bernard frowned. "I know you have a weapon. Put it on the ground."

Alex extracted his revolver and carefully laid it at his feet.

"Now step away from it." Bernard waved his gun.

Alex stepped to the side and raised his arms. His stomach twisted as he watched Bernard approach.

"Tell me, *Maurice*," Alex said, "how are the wedding plans coming along?"

Bernard halted and scowled.

"I'm sure Annabelle's eagerly awaiting the nuptials. Is that why you want me so bad, as a trophy for your wife-to-be?"

"Don't dare speak to me about that woman." Bernard's face flushed.

Alex took a step back. Could there be trouble between them?

"If you must know, the bitch called off the wedding."

Alex frowned. "She does have a habit of doing that. Surely it wasn't just because you allowed me to escape."

Bernard's face grew redder.

Alex kept a wary eye on the revolver that shook in the captain's hand.

"She called it off because of you."

"I fear I don't understand."

"When she heard the tale of your capture and daring escape, she decided she'd made a mistake in jilting you. She has this fool notion she can win you back. After she saw you in camp is what did it. I'll forever curse that woman for not turning you in then."

Alex felt like laughing. Annabelle had never been logical in her decisions, but he had to wonder what her family thought of this crazy scheme.

"She'll never win me back. I'm done with her."

"But you're still the reason she's jilted me."

Alex shook his head. "Annabelle is fickle. You can try to reason with her, but I'm sure you could do much better."

Bernard's face hardened. "As you well know, her family is quite wealthy. Because of you, I've lost out, and somebody's going to pay. It may as well be you." He raised his revolver.

Alex stiffened. He had a pistol in his vest pocket but didn't think he'd have time to reach for it.

A shotgun blast rang out. Startled, Alex glanced behind him.

Katie stood at the base of the porch, a smoking rifle in her arms. "Ye'll not be taking him anywhere, Bernard."

Alex's blood heated. "I told you to go inside."

Bernard laughed. "I can just as easily take both of you, and you'll end up in prison together. Or maybe you'd both like to hang."

"And I can easily shoot you where you stand." Katie's face hardened.

This situation was rapidly growing beyond

Alex's control, but he used the distraction to extract his pistol, hiding it under the tail of his frock coat. Wanting Katie safe inside with her baby, he tried to appeal to her again.

"Katie..." A click froze him.

He turned his gaze to Bernard. The captain scowled, his revolver leveled at Alex.

Before Alex could raise his pistol, a loud blast sounded and Bernard flew backward, his arms outstretched. Alex looked back at Katie. She still held the rifle, her face pale.

"Make sure the devil's dead," she ordered.

Alex swallowed, then nodded. He gingerly approached Bernard. The man didn't move. He picked up Bernard's revolver then inspected the body. Katie's shot had gone right through the center of his chest. Glancing back at her, he nodded. "He's gone."

Katie lowered the rifle, her sigh of relief audible.

Tenants emerged from the house to see what the shots were about. Katie explained the man had tried to take Isabel and had threatened her friend and herself, so she'd had no choice but to shoot.

Alex reached her side, taking the rifle and propping it against the porch railing.

"I told him I'd kill him if he tried to hurt me child."

Alex took her into his arms, reveling in her softness and sweet scent. She leaned into him for a few heavenly moments, then stiffened.

"I'm thinking you should be on yer way." She gazed at him sadly.

"But..."

"The authorities will come to investigate. It wouldn't be wise fer you to stay."

"I can't just leave you to deal with this."

She shrugged. "Me landlady will back up me story that he tried to harm Isabel. And the other

211

tenants know me as well. I'll be fine." She held his gaze. "Ye'd best go."

He nodded, knowing she was right. He glanced at the tenants milling around Bernard's body. A few were young men. He wondered if she'd lied about Isabel's father being gone. Could one of them be him?

He kissed Katie's cheek in farewell, then turned away. Pain gripped his chest, and he feared he'd collapse. She and her child were safe now. He had to go on with his life and forget her.

Chapter Twenty-Four

Virginia boardinghouse
Christmas Day, 1864

After helping Mrs. Borden prepare the house for Christmas, Katie felt exhausted. Isabel was now ten months old and very active. Balancing her work at the boardinghouse and caring for the child proved difficult, but she wouldn't give her little angel up for the world. Mrs. Borden assisted with Isabel's care whenever she could, and a few of the borders helped out, too.

The incident with Bernard last fall was investigated, but Katie wasn't held because the army officials concluded Bernard had been troubled by being jilted by his fiancée and the matter was dismissed.

Although Mrs. Borden had planned to put up a small tabletop tree, one of the male borders had trimmed a huge Christmas tree and lugged it into the parlor. All of the tenants had gotten into the spirit. They contributed time and material to decorate and make the house festive.

The borders planned to make merry despite the country being in the fourth year of the war. Katie tried to keep up her holiday spirit but couldn't shake her melancholy mood.

She settled on the settee in the parlor to complete the sweater she'd been knitting for Isabel in her spare time. The child had been put to bed for the night. She started on her task and let out a long, loud sigh.

"Can't sleep, dear?"

Startled, she glanced up to see Mrs. Borden framed in the doorway.

"I didn't mean to frighten you." She settled her ample frame on the rocking chair by the fireplace.

Katie shook her head. "'Tis all right. I thought everyone had gone to bed by now."

"As you should be." Mrs. Borden nodded toward Katie's lap. "Knitting always settles me when I've got worries. Is there anything I can help you with?"

"No, thank you." Katie concentrated on her project.

"I don't mean to pry into your affairs, but sometimes it helps if you talk over your troubles."

Katie set down her knitting and eyed Mrs. Borden. In all her months here, the woman had been nothing but kind to her. She reminded her of her grandmother in Ireland.

"The man who was here last summer..." Katie began.

"The handsome gentleman?" Mrs. Borden's lips curved into a smile. "He was more than just an acquaintance of yours, I take it."

"I loved him, but I felt unable to share a life with him."

"I see." Mrs. Borden watched her.

"You see, I discovered he was a Yankee spy. I didn't know this when we first met, but by the time I found out—"

"You'd fallen for him."

"Aye." Katie nodded, so relieved to get this off her chest. "I tried to turn him in but ended up setting him free."

"You were a woman in love. And he seemed like such a fine gentleman." The landlady shook her head.

"That's just it. He is a fine, upstanding man. And he had good reason for doing what he did. I couldn't fault him."

"Well, after meeting him, I can't say I blame you for being smitten."

"I fear I've made a terrible mistake." Katie stared at her hands sitting idly in her lap.

"Why is that, dear?"

"After I left him two summers ago, I thought to never see him again."

Mrs. Borden nodded, comprehension dawning. "He tracked you down."

"Aye. I fear I drove him away again."

The landlady settled back and sighed. "It's so hard to believe such a handsome gentleman is a Yankee spy. No wonder you were taken in."

"Aye. But now I fear I should have been truthful with him."

"You still love him?"

Katie nodded.

"Then, child, you've got to find him, no matter how, and tell him so."

"Even though he's a Yankee?"

"This war will come to an end sooner or later. In time, it won't matter which side of the fence you were on. You've got to follow your heart." She rose and patted Katie's hands. "Do whatever your heart tells you to do."

****

Petersburg, Virginia
March 1, 1865

Alex crouched at the edge of a long trench the soldiers had dug. They faced the trenches the Rebels occupied surrounding Petersburg. The Union Army had the Confederates trapped but still they held out, even though they were unable to get supplies in or out through Union lines.

Over the winter months, life in the trenches was harsh, cold, and filthy. Many men had succumbed to illness and death. Unlike the Rebels, though, Union soldiers received good rations and decent clothing.

After Katie's betrayal last summer, Alex had resigned his commission as a Federal spy and now served as an infantry captain. He wanted to serve out his time in the uniform of his chosen side. If he survived the war, he'd settle in the north and start life over.

"Captain." An aide approached from behind. "The colonel wishes to brief you. If you could accompany me back to headquarters."

The Federal Army had set up their headquarters in tents about a quarter mile beyond the trenches, well out of the range of Rebel artillery.

"Very well, Corporal." Alex rose to his feet with a grunt. A barrage of rifle fire sent the aide scurrying behind a wide tree trunk. Alex dove to the ground, but not before he felt something rip through his upper back, below his right shoulder blade.

"Damnation!" he gasped as he realized the Rebels had gotten him *again*.

****

Alex woke lying on his stomach. Doctors and nurses bustled about him. As consciousness returned, so did pain. He tried to move, wincing at the effort, but sharp tearing in his shoulder forced him to lie still.

"Alex?"

He opened his eyes to find Elliot standing over him.

"I thought you were in Washington," Alex murmured.

"I was until I received orders to report here. I didn't know you were back in the ranks."

"Thought it best." Alex gritted his teeth as pain shot through his shoulder. "Got tired of all the lies."

Elliot nodded. "I assume you never found Miss Katie."

"I found her a year ago living in a boardinghouse

just outside Culpepper."

"You don't say. Is she still there?"

"Wouldn't know...and don't care."

"Things ended badly, I take it." Elliot frowned.

"She's moved on. Has a child by another man." The pain and regret returned, making his physical pain seem trifling.

"Sorry to hear that, friend. I had hoped she was the one for you."

After a brief examination of the wound, Elliot said, "It doesn't look too bad. I'll clean it out and stitch you up, and you'll be good as new once it's healed."

Alex waited for Elliot to return, his thoughts drifting to Katie. He'd thought, after the travesty of Annabelle, that Katie was the woman for him. Even with all their differences, he'd truly loved her.

Now, he didn't know if he could ever love or trust a woman again.

****

Virginia boardinghouse
March 12, 1865

Katie sat in the parlor with Mrs. Borden enjoying a cup of tea. They watched Isabel toddle across the floor. The baby settled into Katie's waiting arms, clapping her chubby little hands.

Mr. Washman, one of the tenants, peered into the room. "Did you all hear the news?" he drawled.

After exchanging a puzzled glance with Mrs. Borden, Katie shook her head.

Her landlady said, "No, sir. What's happened?"

"Lincoln's taken office for his second term. Disgusting is all I can say."

"Amen to that," Mrs. Borden agreed.

Katie kept her silence. The politics of her adopted country no longer interested her. She wished the war would end and didn't care any longer which side won. What did it matter to her? Except for Isabel, she'd lost everything she'd ever cared about.

She was ready to start life over.

After Mr. Washman had gone to his room, Mrs. Borden eyed Katie. "You look troubled, dear."

"I've just been thinking of all the people I've lost since the war started."

"I'm sure you're missing little Isabel's father." Mrs. Borden nodded. "It's a real pity when a father can never lay eyes on his child."

"Aye," Katie agreed. She felt somewhat guilty. Mrs. Borden was, of course, referring to Rory. Attempting to change the subject, she said, "Me husband's brother was killed during the battle at Gettysburg."

The landlady nodded, sympathy in her eyes. "You have no other family?"

Katie shook her head. "Me parents died in the slums of New York City, and I haven't heard from me brothers for over a year. They went out west to escape the draft."

"What about your gentleman friend?"

"The Yankee spy?" Katie smiled, surprised Mrs. Borden, a loyal Confederate, wouldn't be repelled at the thought of her being courted by a Yankee.

"If he's an honorable man, don't let him go. Your child needs a father."

Katie set Isabel on the floor and sat back, her thoughts turning inward. Of course, she had never admitted to Mrs. Borden Alex was Isabel's father. But her landlady was right. She couldn't keep Alex from knowing he'd fathered a child. No matter what her own feelings were regarding him, it wasn't her place to keep him from Isabel.

She had no idea where Alex was, but knowing him, he'd be right in the thick of things. A plan began to form.

Chapter Twenty-Five

Union camp outside Petersburg, Virginia
March 30, 1865

After months of correspondence, Katie located Dr. Elliot James. She found him stationed outside Petersburg and through him, she learned Alex had been wounded and was recovering in a camp near the battle zone.

At Mrs. Borden's urging, she left Isabel in her landlady's capable hands and traveled south. Giving the doctor's letter to the pickets, she was admitted to the Union camp on the pretext of being a Northern volunteer.

She adjusted her bonnet and smoothed her skirt as she entered the hospital tent. People bustled about, many in blood-stained aprons. Katie clenched her jaw at the familiar though pitiful sight of wounded and ill men scattered about on cots throughout the tent's interior.

"Pardon me." Katie tried to gain someone's attention. "But I'm looking fer Dr. James."

A dark-haired woman whose hair had escaped her bun and coiled over her shoulder, pointed at a spot behind Katie. Before she could thank the woman, she'd hurried off to attend to a soldier's urgent cry.

Katie turned and spied a dark-haired man in a blood-spattered apron leaning over a patient.

"Dr. James." She moved toward him.

He looked up, a smile forming on his thin face. "Miss Katie, such a pleasure to see you again."

She wound her way among the soldiers until she stood face to face with the doctor but stopped when she saw him close the patient's eyes and pull the blanket over his face.

"We've lost this one, I'm afraid."

She bowed her head, not knowing what to say.

The doctor eyed her with concern. "I have news about Alex, however—"

"Oh, no!" Katie stared at him, her pulse throbbing. "Yer not saying he's—he's..." She couldn't get out the words she feared to utter.

"I must apologize, Miss Katie, I never meant to frighten you. Alex is still with us. He's recovered from a slight shoulder wound, but he's developed an infection and has taken a turn for the worse, I fear."

Katie blinked, trying to comprehend. "Where is he?"

"Come with me." Dr. James grasped her arm.

When Dr. James led her to Alex, she gasped, her knees shaking. "Holy Mother of God! What have they done to you?"

She gripped his hand, but he showed no sign he felt her touch. Leaning close, she felt his exhalation against her cheek. She placed her fingers on his throat looking for a pulse. Although she found one, it was light and thready.

Her throat went dry. He couldn't die. She needed to tell him about Isabel. How could she forgive herself for lying to him?

Taking a rag and a basin of water, she sponged the sweat from his face. His normally suntanned skin looked pale as death.

Gripping his hand in both of hers, she prayed for him to live.

"Don't you be dying on me, Alex Hart. I'll never forgive you if you do."

She stayed by his side until Dr. James ordered her to lie down on one of the empty cots and get some rest.

****

April 5, 1865

Alex woke from a dream. He'd stood on the long, wraparound porch of his family's plantation house, surveying the bright, tranquil day. The day he'd returned from his semester at the university in York, Pennsylvania. He hadn't seen Annabelle in months, although they'd exchanged letters on a regular basis, since he'd gone up north. They were to be married in a few months, and she asked to meet to discuss wedding plans.

During his last semester, Fort Sumter had been attacked and the State of Virginia had seceded from the Union a few days later, following the lead of other States. Once he returned home, he realized Annabelle, as well as his family, expected him to enlist in the Confederate Army.

Annabelle shed tears when he rejected the commission his father had set up for him. She wanted the prestige of being the wife of a Confederate officer, not the shame of being wed to a shirker.

Sighing, he glanced around the medical tent. He was still weak as a kitten. One of the female, nurse volunteers brought him a cup of water to ease his parched throat.

Recalling the dream, he realized he'd never loved Annabelle. His family had deemed them a good match and encouraged him to court her. Their breakup, though it had hurt him deeply at the time, had been for the best. He never would have been happy with her or fighting for a cause he didn't believe in.

And he never would have met Katie.

She was the strongest woman he'd ever known. She'd had to overcome so much. But memories of their lovemaking, brought back her softness and sweetness.

Damn this war! They were on opposite sides just as he and Annabelle had been. No possible way could he hope to have a life with the headstrong Rebel.

But unlike Annabelle, he truly loved Katie and would never forget her.

He drifted back to sleep.

When he woke, Katie stood over him.

****

Katie hovered over Alex, praying he'd awaken. He'd been drifting in and out of consciousness for days. Dr. James assured her he was strong and should recover with time. She had to tell him how she felt and about his daughter, but he hadn't as yet seemed to recognize her.

He stirred and his eyes popped open. She took his hand. "Alex!"

Frowning, he stared at her a moment, then his lips curved into a smile. "Katie? Am I dreaming, or is it really you?"

"Aye. 'Tis me. But I thought you'd never want to see me again."

His brow furrowed as if he were trying to make sense of what she said. She smoothed the crease in his brow with her fingertips and sighed.

"'Tis something I must tell you about Isabel."

"Your daughter," he rasped.

"Our daughter." She watched his reaction.

His eyes widened. "Isabel is...is..."

Katie nodded. "She's yours."

"I have a daughter?"

Katie laughed, but the laugh died in her throat. Alex's eyes rolled back, and his eyelids fluttered. Holding tight to his hand, she tried to bring him back.

"I love you, Alex. You can't leave me now. You can't leave Isabel. Come back."

She turned cold with fear.
She shook him, but he didn't wake.
Was he dying?
"Dr. James!" she screamed.

Chapter Twenty-Six

April 9, 1865

Alex felt he'd been drifting through haze. The sensation was like swimming underwater. He kept kicking for the surface and the light. When he broke the surface, a form hovered over him surrounded by a golden glow.

An angel.

His vision cleared. He found himself looking into a pair of beautiful, gray eyes. Katie's cheeks glistened with tears.

He tried to speak, but his voice wouldn't come. She leaned down and stroked his brow, her touch cool and soothing. She offered him water. The cool liquid slid down his throat, loosening his parched vocal chords.

She took his hand, kissing his fingertips. The soft tingle of her full lips sent a delightful shiver through him.

"Why are you crying?" he asked.

"I thought I'd lost you."

A sudden memory from last summer returned to him. "You told me the child wasn't mine. Why did you lie?"

Her forehead creased. Pain flitted across her eyes. "I thought I wanted to move on without you. If I'd have told you the truth, you wouldn't have stayed away."

"And why have you told me now?" As much as he wanted her, he had to wonder at her sudden change of attitude. After all, nothing had changed.

They still remained on opposite sides of this conflict.

She bit her lip. "I've had a lot of time to think. You weren't responsible fer what happened to me family. And ye've given me Isabel. After losing me first child, I feared I'd never have the chance to have another babe."

He eyed her with doubt. Was it just because of the child that she needed him now—a way for her to gain respectability—or a means of support?

"It seems to me," he said, "that you only tell the truth when it suits your purpose to do so."

Her brow creased. Pain dulled her eyes. "I wanted to keep our daughter away from the conflict. I left the army fer good while you were still spying fer the Yankees. Now you wear their uniform."

"I'm sorry you weren't able to put politics aside for the sake of our daughter." Anger bubbled inside him at what she'd denied him.

"'Tis for her sake that I'm telling you now." She turned away and strode from the tent.

Elliot approached. "You know," he said, "she's spent the past few days at your bedside. Refused to leave even though I threatened to throw her out if she didn't take some rest. If that isn't love, by God, I don't know what is."

"Damnation," Alex said. "Why does everything have to be so hard?"

****

Katie sat on a stool outside the tent with her shawl wrapped around her to ward off the early morning chill. Dabbing at her eyes, she tried to fathom where she'd gone wrong. After nearly dying, she'd thought he'd be happy to know Isabel was his.

Aware of a presence standing over her, she glanced up into Dr. James' concerned eyes. He rested a comforting hand on her shoulder.

"You need to give him more time to absorb the information," he said. "He told me you'd had a child

225

with another man. That hurt him deeply."

"Aye," Katie said. "That's what I told him. At the time I thought it best to keep him away. Everyone thought the baby to be me late husband's, but Alex knew that to be impossible."

"He feels betrayed. First by your admission of being with another man, then by your lies."

She nodded, bowing her head in shame. "I can't blame him for hatin' me, but I don't want him to hate Isabel."

Dr. James sighed. "Allow me to speak to him. Perhaps I can talk him into being reasonable."

Katie nodded again, as hope rose. In the end, though, she decided it would be for the best if she left without seeing him and returned home to Isabel. Alex would never love her after all her lies. How could he ever trust her? She'd raise her child as any widowed mother would. This war had left so many children fatherless. Love was just not an option for her.

Gathering her shawl about her, she rose, planning to leave before Dr. James returned. She wanted nothing with Alex if he didn't want her or his daughter. Wiping a tear from her cheek, she took a few steps, but a hand on her arm stopped her.

"Miss Katie," Dr. James said, "Alex wants to see you."

****

Alex sat propped against pillows, sipping beef broth. Once Elliot had convinced him to keep Katie from leaving, he worried she wouldn't want to see him after the callous way he'd driven her off.

She frowned as she approached, her face streaked with tears. But she still looked beautiful. The most beautiful woman he'd ever seen.

She moved slowly toward him, biting her lip. She glanced at Elliot. He nodded, then moved away to give them privacy.

Alex shook his head. "You don't know how lovely you look."

She smoothed her skirt, a wavering smile on her lush lips.

"I look a fright."

"No, you're beautiful. Just like that little girl of yours."

She smiled. "Isabel."

"Yes. Isabel. Our lovely daughter." He reached out to take her hand.

"You believe me, then?"

"From the first time I laid eyes on her, I knew she was mine."

"I should have told you then." She clasped his hand between both of hers. "But I was afraid."

He frowned. "You were afraid of me?"

"You'd lied to me before, and you were the enemy of all I'd fought for."

He held her gaze. "I can't give up what I believe in or what I'm fighting for." He shrugged. "Reckon you'll just have to take me as I am."

Katie's lips curved into a smile. "I already have."

Alex took her hands into both of his, kissing each of her slender palms. She gazed at him with such longing. He made his decision.

"Would you ever consider having a Virginia Yankee for a husband?"

Her eyes sparkled. She swayed her hips, a smile playing about her lips. "Well, I wouldn't be knowing, sir. That would depend on the gentleman in question."

"It would, would it?" He pulled her toward him. "And how would you come to your decision?" He wrapped his arms around her slim waist.

"It depends on how well he kisses."

He grinned. "Reckon I'll have to demonstrate." Taking her mouth, he thrilled to the feel of the woman of his dreams, the mother of his child, warm and vibrant in his arms.

When they broke from the kiss, he turned to find Elliot grinning at them.

"I see all is well here," Elliot said.

"Not quite," Alex said, not letting go of Katie's waist. "We'll be needing a preacher...and a witness. Would you do us the honor?"

Elliot grinned. "Be more than happy to, my friend."

Epilogue

York, Pennsylvania
April 30, 1866

Katie adjusted her wrapper as another swift kick assured her the babe she carried was doing well. She patted her swollen abdomen then lumbered after Isabel as she raced on her toes across the kitchen floor.

At the sound of the front door opening, she took her daughter by the hand, propelling her along to the entry way. Alex stood in the door with an armload of books.

"And how was yer first day of university?" she asked.

He dropped the pile of books on the table. "It's different when you're the teacher. I liked it just fine."

Katie smiled. Isabel toddled over to her father. He scooped her up and transferred her to one arm. His other hand he placed on Katie's protruding stomach.

"And how is our son today?"

Katie grinned. Because the baby was so active, they'd decided it must be a boy.

"The little lad has been kicking all day long. I hope fer sure he'll tire out soon."

Alex smiled when a foot pressed against his hand.

"You see?" Katie said.

Alex put his arm around her shoulder and propelled her, with Isabel in his other arm, to the parlor where they sat huddled together on the settee.

"I'm looking forward to our future adventures together, Mrs. Hart."

Katie patted her stomach. "Aye. And to many more to come."

Alex leaned over capturing her mouth as Isabel giggled.

Katie's lips tingled, and her body heated as always when her husband kissed her. Her battles were finally over.

About the author...

Susan Macatee has been writing toward publication since 1995. Her romance stories focus on the paranormal and history, particularly the American Civil War era.

Her main focus at present is Civil War romance. Her interest in the time period stems from her husband getting involved with the 28th Pennsylvania Regiment Civil War reenacting group and pulling her right in.

Her other love is sci-fi, which she reads voraciously and hopes to incorporate into future romance plots. She lives with her husband and three grown sons, as well as the family dog, a female boxer named Kelly. She spends her free time watching her local baseball team, the Philadelphia Phillies, inhaling books and baking.

Visit Susan at www.susanmacatee.com